DEPRAVED
A PLEASURE & PREY NOVEL

AJ MERLIN

Depraved

Copyright © 2022 AJ Merlin

All Rights Reserved

No part of this book may be reproduced in any form or by any electronic or mechanical means, including information storage and retrieval systems, without written permission from the author, except for the use of brief quotations in a book review.

Cover Design by Books and Moods

Ebook ISBN: 978-1-955540-13-1

Paperback ISBN: 978-1-955540-14-8

AUTHOR'S NOTE

Depraved is a dark, fast-burn romance. If you're troubled by kinks such as primal, CNC, or knife-play, it might not be for you. Also there is a little bit of dubious consent, but Sloane is *always* allowed to make her own, informed choice in things. There is very minimal animal cruelty in one scene, and Sloane's love interest is not someone any of us would bring home to meet our parents.

...Hopefully.

And never fear–the dogs don't die.

1

Do I know any good scary stories? I stare at the fire in front of me, drawing one leg up in the wide seat of the camp chair poised on one side of the flames. Gravel crunches under my other foot as I slide it back and forth, eyes still fixed on the flames of the campfire as I consider the question.

"Do you?" Harriet's son, Oliver, is just as impatient as his mother, though not nearly as charming. He squirms in his chair across from the crackling fire, and when his father, Benjamin, hears the noise from the deck they've built onto their impressive camper, he glances up from cleaning the grill to check that everything is fine.

At my side, the large, mostly black German Shepherd thumps his tail on the ground as if to reassure Benjamin everything is fine. My other Shepherd, who is tanner and fluffier than his counterpart, sits between the two children across the fire, letting them pet his furry head while his tongue lolls and his eyes remain on me.

I can still task, Mom, his eyes seem to say. *The moment you need me, I'll jump this fire and be in your lap in an instant.*

Not that my chubbier, lazier Shepherd is going to be jumping fires anytime soon.

"I..." I trail off thoughtfully, biting my lower lip and sawing my teeth against it. "Do horror movies count?" I ask finally, letting out a soft, apologetic laugh to accompany the words.

"Mom and Dad won't let us watch horror movies," Emily informs me matter-of-factly. "She says we aren't old enough."

"You probably aren't," I tell them, nodding sagely. I'm not sure how old they are, exactly. They've been camping in Oak Crest longer than I've been working or living here myself.

"They count, then," Oliver encourages, dropping his legs over the front of his too-big chair as Argus pants and flicks an ear back, utterly relaxed but still aware of the situation around us. My fluffy Shepherd is amazing with kids, though I guess I shouldn't be surprised. His trainer made sure that he was good with anything and everything, and kids were high on the list of things to get him used to.

I'm also pretty sure Argus *loves* children.

As opposed to my non-service dog, Vulcan, who sighs and shifts on the ground beside me. The mostly black dog barely looks anything like Argus, with shorter fur and a more muscular, lean build. His personality is just as dissimilar as the rest of him. Vulcan is more of a guard dog than anything, even if one of his favorite hobbies is snoring on the end of my bed while sleeping like a cockroach.

"Your parents will *kill* me if I describe horror movies in any kind of detail to you," I snort, unable to help imagining the two kids petrified in their camper while their parents are trying to sleep.

"And neither of you will be able to sleep for weeks if she does." Harriet's footsteps crunch on the gravel as she walks towards the fire, s'mores fixings in hand. "Are you staying for s'mores, Sloane?" she asks, casting a warm smile in my direction.

I hesitate, considering, but I've known for a few minutes that I need to go back to my cabin. I'm *tired*, for one. More tired than I should be, but after having a massive panic attack this morning that Argus had to help pull me out of but still almost keep me in bed, I really just want to vegetate in my own cabin and fall asleep to whatever Hulu has first on my lineup.

"Nah," I say, pushing myself to my feet with a sigh. Beside me, Vulcan is on his paws instantly as well, staring up at me with the same level of attachment, though with more intensity than Argus usually shows. While Vulcan will never task for me, alert me to any kind of episode I'm about to have, or do any of the things Argus is trained for in a bad situation, I love him all the same. And he's just as much an integral part of *Team Sloane* as Argus is. Without him, I wouldn't feel as safe as I do, rolling up on drunk campers or investigating big-animal-like sounds in the woods.

Okay, I still don't investigate scary sounds for the most part. Normally I chicken out and call the Oak Crest owners, who live *literally* over the hill from the campground and are on call 24-7, just like I am.

I'm just the first line of defense, seeing as I stay *in* the campground and all.

Argus is at my side only a second later, tail wagging, as I reach down to absently stroke his soft, fluffy ears. His tongue still lolls, and he's warm from the campfire.

"We'll be up at the house tomorrow to talk to Pat and Sam about the additions we're looking to do," Benjamin adds, toweling off his hands before giving me a quick wave. "And make sure you're back here on Thursday. We're moving up BBQ night so that Carter can show up."

"Carter, huh?" I stretch my arms over my head, my ponytail pulling slightly and causing my scalp to ache. "Did you have to *bribe* him to get him to show up?" The middle-aged man is just as old as the owners and has been coming here for as long as they've owned it, I'm sure. He's also notoriously anti-social and turns down most invitations by the regulars to show up for dinner.

Benjamin beams. "Something like that," he chuckles, hands in his pockets. "Have a good night."

"G'night, Sloane," Harriet calls when I set my foot on the pavement of the road that loops around to all the campsites in one way or another.

"Good night!" I shout back, not bothering to call either dog to me or worry about a leash. They've been living here with me for the year and a half that I've worked on-site for Oak Crest. They know their way around better than me, and neither of them has ever shown any interest in leaving my side when we walk.

My only complaint tonight is how far I am from home. The campground is a pretty good size, probably a mile and a half or so from the lake to the farthest campsite or cabin. Most of it sits close to Colidale Lake, and there are two different boat launches for the busy season.

Currently, it is *not* prime-time. Even in mid-April, though, we're still surprisingly full of campers who've stampeded down from Akron, Ohio, which is only about thirty miles northeast, or locals from Arkala, Ohio, nearby. Woe betide anyone to tell them the lake is fucking *freezing* right now, or that the wind blowing off it can get *cold*. Sure, you might get lucky and get a seventy-five-degree day and fifty-five-degree night. But it's more likely that our weather will sock you in the face with rain, bad temperatures, and water so choppy it looks like it could *eat* you.

I shiver in my light hoodie, shoving my hands in my pockets as I turn the corner and walk up the slight incline that leads away from the House, which is what we call the office and camp store, and towards the more-wooded rear area of the campground. Back here, trees obscure more and more of the area and stand at attention behind the campsites, behind them is the utter blackness of the forest we're located within.

I like it...most of the time.

But there's no denying that it's a little *eerie* back here. And could turn into a scary situation real quick in the winter, when there's almost no one here and everything is snowed in.

Luckily, in the winter, I still have power here. And the campground is never truly empty. There are a few people, like Carter, who live here year-round, as I do.

Crickets sound off, along with the other insects and small animals that call the trees around here home, I sigh as I walk, legs straining as the ground slants upward once more. It's not the hilliest hill on the campground; the one leading to the lakeside cabins is *much* worse. But the slow, increasing gradient is a workout all on its own, especially when I do this almost every night when I head back to my cabin.

On my left, in the radius of one of the street lamps that line the asphalt, I pass the big, sculpted tree that's made to look like a rearing bear. Once upon a time, it must've truly been a *massive* tree. But the trunk that's left behind now is about eight feet tall, and it would take five of me to link arms around the circumference of the bear that stands with its mouth open and one paw raised as if to strike.

I've seen it a thousand times before. I've touched it and stood on my tiptoes to poke the fur of its chest. Tonight I barely glance at it as I walk by.

To my surprise, Vulcan slows to a stop at my side, head

tilted quizzically as his ears rotate like satellites towards the tree.

I slow as well, and at my side Argus gazes at me with rapt attention. He couldn't care less about whatever has caught Vulcan's attention, though I stop in the road to let my guard dog figure out what's so interesting about the tree.

"It's the bear tree, Vulc," I remind him when he doesn't move. He doesn't look at me, instead tilts his head to the other side before finally walking away from the spot and further up the hill, as if there was never anything there at all.

But I look at it again anyway, eyes following the curves of fur and legs until I get to the face that snarls silently towards the road.

It's just the bear tree.

There are no sounds in the night around me out of the ordinary. Nothing that would tip me off to something *else* being here or anyone off in the woods later than they really should be. There are snakes in the woods. Not to mention ticks, spiders, and the occasional predator. I don't know why anyone would want to be out there without a light.

Suddenly Argus nudges my hand hard, and I rest it on his ears again as my heart picks up just a little in my chest. There's *nothing* out there, I repeat in my head, barely noticing him nudge my hand once more.

It's just the bear tree.

But for some reason tonight, that doesn't make my heart slow. It doesn't stop the sudden, unwelcome rush of memory that has *nothing* to do with the campground or the tree. It doesn't stop my mouth from almost moving to shape the word that I screamed so hard and so often when I was eleven.

Help.

Help me.

Help–

Without warning, Argus rears up and presses his paws against my chest, tongue finding my face as he frantically washes my cheek and nose. He holds himself up for the most part, though my hands find his elbows to support him as he wags his tail and continues to wash my face.

"Okay, okay. *Break*," I tell him, giving him his command so that he'll stop actively tasking for me.

Instantly, Argus drops to my side and sits, caramel eyes still watching my face. *I'll do it again*; he seems to say, *if you start that again.*

It's not my intention to start anything again.

I take off at a quicker pace, forcing my stiff legs into an almost-jog as I go up the hill, around the two campsites that are taken for the first time this year, and back to the farthest part of the campground, the cabin in the woods.

It's got its own little driveway, and here the incline gets a bit steeper as the road narrows to one-car-only. My car sits in front of the porch, parked diagonally across the pavement because I *can*, and I walk past it to stand on the porch in the light of the lamp above the door, where moths flitter and flip around the bulb.

I'm home. The wooden rails around the long porch are comforting, as is the familiarity of my little cabin.

The dogs must think so as well. Vulcan stalks off to my left, going behind the cabin to where the fire pit, grill, and picnic table sit. I don't often use the grill. I had never learned exactly the dos and don'ts of using one, and the propane tank under it makes me slightly nervous, even though I'm twenty-seven and can use an oven *just fine*.

It's just not the same, though.

I *do* use the fire pit at least three times a week. I love campfires, and not just in the s'mores way. Fires are great. Plus, in the summer, they're a great way to keep the mosquitos away while I'm hanging out at the cabin.

"Go on," I tell Argus, stepping back onto the pavement and walking towards the backside of the cabin. I flick on a switch on the side of the building as I go, and a string of fairy lights that hang on the porch come on instantly, their warm glow illuminating the area just a bit further than my porch light. "You gotta pee before we go in. I don't want to get up in three hours." He doesn't actually need to go out in the middle of the night, normally. He's good at holding it. But I don't want him to have to if I can help it.

Vulcan, on the other hand, would probably break the door down himself, or leap out a window like some police dog, if I didn't get up fast enough to let him out. The darker German Shepherd prowls around the edge of the lot, nose to the ground just over the ditch that lines the woods on either side of me.

This place *used* to be rented out, like the other cabins that sit closer to the lake across the campground. It was popular because of how isolated it is. But that's part of the problem. After a few unsavory campers made a mess of the place and did a lot of shit they weren't supposed to back here, the owners decided it wasn't worth it to offer up such an isolated spot.

It's only forty feet from the nearest campsite, though even that one isn't requested *too* much. So outside of the really popular times of summer, I'm normally pretty alone back here.

Not that I mind. It's quite nice, honestly.

Argus follows Vulcan around the perimeter, though my service dog looks more like a bouncing teddy bear than anything that'll rip someone's face off as Vulcan does. Neither of them is particularly vicious. Nor have they ever bit anyone for any reason at all.

The worst that Vulcan does is bark to scare off coyotes, and normally Argus will chime in with his own brand of German Shepherd Intimidation.

"C'mon boys," I say, whistling to get their attention. Argus pulls away, walking to the door and putting his nose against it to tell me he's *more* than ready to get back to our air-conditioned home. He's not a creature that's made for the outdoors. Or strife. Or hiking.

Or any adversity, really.

Vulcan, however, stares off at the woods behind the cabin. His tail is stiff behind him, and he tilts his head to the side once more, like there's something back there that's caught his interest.

I suck in a breath, fighting the urge to let my imagination wander. That's one thing I've had to work on since moving here. It's easy to see shapes in the dark and hear noises that aren't really there when there's no light to illuminate the woods around me. Especially for someone like me, who already struggles with a real issue of panicking and paranoia.

"What's wrong, Vulcan?" I snort, going to the side of the porch and leaning over the rail. There's no movement past the fire pit or the back of the house, just trees, trees, and more trees. Without any wind, it's completely still and uninteresting.

And I *refuse* to see anything that isn't there. Sucking in a breath, I turn to look at my dog, who's looking at me now instead of the trees.

"Come *on*," I urge, going to the door and opening it. "There's nothing there."

Vulcan wags his tail slightly, uncertainly even, before following me into the cabin where I close and lock the door behind both dogs and myself before letting out a breath I didn't know I'd been holding.

There's nothing out there.

I hate that I have to repeat that to myself. I *despise* that this morning's episode has me so on edge. Not to mention the bit of panic by the bear tree that Argus pushed me to recognize only a few minutes ago.

Instinctively, I flip on the lights, illuminating the main room of the cabin. To my left sits an open door to the bedroom that used to hold two full beds. Now my room is there, decorated much more to *my* taste than the rustic-camping theme it used to have.

In front of me, the bathroom door is open, and from inside, I hear the heater kick on. I don't have a tub. Only a large shower, but frankly, the bathroom is perfect for me. To my right sits a large, plush sofa, and across from it, a television on top of a glass stand. I still have no idea how nothing has ever happened to the TV, especially with two giant dogs living here. But it's still kicking, and I'm pretty sure I've found the sweet spot for it. Therefore, I'm never going to move it or anything else in the room. Not when it's so *perfectly perfect* in terms of stability. I hope.

Finally, around the corner from that is the itty bitty kitchen of the cabin. Only a few feet from the sofa, in front of a window, sits a two-person table where I usually eat and the few appliances that I have. Given that I *suck* at cooking and eat way more frozen or pre-prepared food than any person should, it's fine for me. I'm not cooking anything gourmet or anything that requires more than one small countertop, the stove, the oven, or the microwave.

Honestly, I mostly just use the oven and the microwave. Or the fire outside, when I'm grilling hotdogs or sandwiches over it as I prefer.

Some people might call it *lazy*. I just like to think I'm simple and easy to please. And way too addicted to campfire food.

Absently, I pick up the dogs' water bowl from the mat,

dump it out, and refill it in the kitchen sink. It's the only sound in the cabin, apart from the heater, and I glance out the window that faces the woods as I lean against the sink.

The trees are still just *trees*.

And I'm still a jumpy, anxious woman who probably needs a new therapist. In the window, I catch sight of my reflection and give a one-sided frown. I look tired, even though I can't *clearly* see my heterochromatic blue and brown eyes. My auburn hair is still high in its ponytail, though wisps have escaped and hang around my pale face. When I'd first moved to the campground, I'd been *sure* I'd lose weight. I'd even told my mom that in a year, I'd probably drop at least a size and fit back into my few pairs of size-fourteen jeans. Instead of the sixteens and eighteens, I wear now.

Somehow, that hasn't happened. I'm not hung up about it, and when Mom asks if I *have* slimmed down enough to fit into them, I sigh and tell her I'm clearly building too much muscle by walking around the campground all day or by helping out with all the things that go into the upkeep of Oak Crest.

I *don't* tell her about all the marshmallows, hot dogs, and slushies I get from the House. Better that she believes that I'm just too *muscular* rather than me admitting that I have a bit of an addiction to a few rather unhealthy foods.

Oh well. What she doesn't know won't hurt her and *certainly* won't hurt me since I have no problem with the way I look. With my luck, if I did lose weight, I'd lose it from my tits or my ass instead of from my stomach or upper arms. Shrinkage of my d-cup girls would be an absolute *tragedy* I'm not willing to risk.

Blinking, I realize that the water is running over the sides of the dog bowl, and I turn with a huff to grab the bowl and set it back on the floor. Argus sniffs it, gives a few licks, and then turns and walks off into the bedroom after Vulcan. I'm sure that my fierce, terrifying guard dog is already stretched out over my queen-size bed, and I know that I'm going to have to fight both of them for the *privilege* of sleeping in *my* own bed unless I fall asleep out here on the sofa, instead.

"Love you guys," I mutter, sinking onto the sofa and grabbing the remote for the TV. In a few button-presses, I'm looking at the Hulu startup screen, and I drag a spare comforter over myself as I settle back against the blush sofa, glad that I can keep a pillow and blanket out here without being judged.

Not like I have any visitors, after all. Nor anyone who might judge me for falling asleep on the sofa instead of on my bed like I probably should.

2

The nose nudging my face while its owner *breathes* against my ear is absolutely unwelcome in every single way imaginable.

The only light in the cabin as I crack my eyes open comes from the television, which currently displays a screen asking me if I'm still watching *whatever* I'd been watching in the first place.

"I'm up, Vulcan," I mutter, barely believing that he needs to go out again tonight. Hadn't he peed when we'd gotten back to the cabin a few hours ago?

A quick glance at my phone shows that it's nearly four in the morning, and I stumble to my feet, clothing askew, before going to the door and pulling it open. I flick the porch light on as Vulcan strides out the door, but instead of following him, I walk to my bedroom, where Argus stares at me from his spot on my canopied bed like *I've* just interrupted *his* sleep without reason.

I hadn't meant to fall asleep in my hoodie and leggings,

and it's not exactly comfy now. Quickly, while I give Vulcan the chance to do what he needs to do, I strip out of my clothes until finally, I'm just in my bra and panties before I go to the window that faces the trees behind the cabin. If my cabin was anywhere else in the campground, I'd never stand in front of an open window while I take my bra off. But there's never anyone back here other than me. And if there were, I'd see some kind of light.

As it is, I try to catch sight of Vulcan from the light streaming out of the window from my room while I pull off my bra and chuck it towards the closet without really caring where it lands. Absently, I reach up to massage the base of my throat, fingers playing over the scar there before I turn and strip off my underwear as well. At least him waking me up means I get to spend the rest of the night in my comfortable pj shorts and a loose tee.

My hair, free from its ponytail even though I don't actually remember taking it down, falls over my shoulders and around my face as I bend down to grab my shorts, and as I stand, I pull them on, my eyes going back to the woods outside the window.

Immediately, I freeze.

Was that something in the trees?

I swear I'd seen something, just for a moment. Like the reflection of light off something shiny or...something?

I walk to the window, belatedly remembering to jerk my t-shirt on over my head and scan the trees outside for *anything*.

But...there's nothing there. Nothing at all. No movement. No light reflecting.

Had it just been an animal, maybe? My light had caught the eyes of a stray raccoon or opossum before. It wouldn't be insane to think the same thing had just happened.

Besides, Vulcan isn't making any kind of noise.

Unless something had dragged him off into the woods.

The thought is irrational and unwelcome. I bolt to the front door and open it, glad no one is around to see me barefoot, with my hair wild around my shoulders and dressed in shorts that barely cover my ass.

"Vulcan?"

He's not barking, but he doesn't come to me immediately, either. I walk to the side of the porch and peer around, and I *think* I can just see his tail somewhere around the back, towards the woods.

"Vulcan?" I call again, leaning further around the porch.

The tail turns out to be a stick, and my heart picks up in my chest as I step onto the asphalt, gritting my teeth against the sharp rock fragments that dig into the bottoms of my feet. The crickets still sing around me, though they seem so *loud* right now as I go around the side of the cabin, trying to dodge around the gravel of the firepit area until I can look behind the house.

He's not there.

"Vulcan!" I call, more loudly this time as my heart trips and stutters in my chest. I shouldn't have let him go out without me. I shouldn't have closed the door or gone back in. Sure, I've done it a thousand times before, and Vulcan has never gone anywhere. But this time–

Underbrush breaks and rustles to my right, and I whirl around just in time to see Vulcan come trotting out of the woods, tail wagging behind him as he licks his mouth like he's just gotten the last slice of pizza.

He's fine. He doesn't even look upset and stares up at me with a tail that continues to wag like he's just had the time of his life in the woods, like always.

"Please tell me you didn't just eat a *rabbit* or something," I mutter, clenching my hands on either side of me, feet braced on the ground just outside of the circle of light from the porch. I glance up, heart still pounding, and let my eyes scan the trees that are just out of reach. The woods get impossibly thick very quickly here, and it wouldn't take more than a dozen steps to get lost.

They're also *eerie* tonight. Though I'm sure it's because of my own racing heart and fear instead of anything *real*.

"You'd tell me if there was anything out here, right Vulc?" I murmur, running my hand over his ears. His tail wags again. He comes closer to stand beside me, pressing against my thigh comfortingly, as if he can sense my unease.

I almost want to call out. I want to ask if anyone's there or even find a light to shine into the woods.

As stupid as that is, anyway. And if I let myself do it once, then I'm really in trouble.

I've worked hard to get myself to be less paranoid, less anxious, and less on edge all the time. I'm not going to let myself take six steps back *now* just because the woods aren't silent, and Vulcan had gone for a little jaunt at four a.m.

"C'mon," I murmur, turning and carefully making my way back to the porch. It's hard to avoid the gravel, and I'm much more aware of the rocks when I find them this time, wincing every time I feel the poke of one in the bottom of my foot. "I can't believe you tried to go on a woods field trip in the freakin' dark," I say as Vulcan walks beside me until he reaches the door and waits, his tail waving like a flag behind him. "But you just really had to scare me like that, huh?" I open the door, having to wait for Argus to move so that I can walk inside. My service dog immediately sniffs my hands, tail wagging once, but I give him the *break* command before he can alert me.

I need to turn things off, and I *know* that I'm freaking out a little. It'll just make me feel worse if he *does* alert me to it.

I quickly lock the door and flip the television off, then go to my bedroom where the light is still on. Vulcan hops up onto my bed and turns in a few circles, pawing at the blankets so he can get them to his liking.

"Uh, I don't think so. You lost solo-bed privileges when you woke me up," I tell him, turning the light off and flipping my phone light on instead.

I locked the door, right?

The thought stops me in my tracks. I shouldn't need to check it. I *did lock it*. I always lock it.

But my brain starts to whisper that maybe, just maybe, I didn't lock it this time, and I should go *check*.

Just this once, I relent silently and walk back to the front door to turn the knob once, twice. Then a third time, just to be sure.

The door is locked, but I stand there and stare at it anyway.

Just to be sure.

As if it's going to *unlock itself* right in front of me.

As if I've hallucinated locking it this whole time, and I'll blink to see that it's sitting open if I stand here long enough.

Again I suck in a breath and tear myself away from the door, hating how aware I am of my feet aching from running around barefoot and how tired I am. My mind feels like it's fraying at the edges, and I go to my bed, shooing Argus out of my spot, and face planting the mattress with a groan.

Frankly, I could probably go to sleep right there. I don't really need to drag myself completely onto the bed. Though, I do. And I barely need a comforter over me with two *radiators* next to the mattress beside me. Vulcan's panting shakes the bed, and fervently I hope that he'll stop sometime before dawn so that the mattress stops making its best impression of one of the vibrating beds from bad old movies that were supposedly once commonly found in motels across America.

Magic Fingers, right? That's what they'd been called.

It doesn't feel very *magic* right now. But it doesn't impede me from falling asleep, one arm over Argus's stomach and front leg as he moves to lie in a line against me, his snores filling the room with a lullaby just as soothing as Vulcan's bed-shaking pants.

3

Pushing the cabin door open as I pocket my phone, I glance up at the pieces of sky that I can see between the leafy branches of the surrounding trees and squint.

It looks a bit like rain. Or like the promise of a storm that's slowly rolling in. I'm surprised that we haven't had more of them lately, with us being on the lake and it being *April* and all. The saying 'April showers bring May flowers' seems to be especially true here in Arkala, but then again, we also get quite a few storms in May as well.

I guess June doesn't rhyme well enough to be used in place of *May*.

Argus and Vulcan roam around the driveway, sniffing at the car and then going to the grass between the trees to do their morning business. While I have a leash on me, just in case, I have no intention of using it. It's been a *long* time since I've used one on either dog while we're at the campground. Both of them, of course, have identifying tags hanging from their collars, and Argus has an extra silver tag that clinks against his name tag and in black letters over a red medical cross, says, SERVICE DOG.

"C'mon," I tell both of them after a minute, locking the cabin door and shoving my keys in the opposite pocket of my denim shorts than my phone. It's warmer than I thought it would be when I was getting dressed, and I'm glad that I put on a light hoodie for the day instead of something heavier. This one zips up to my neck, and the material is clingy, almost spandex in nature. The best part, however, are the thumbholes that I make use of, so the edges of the sleeves go almost to my fingers instead of stopping at my wrist. My beat-up Converse sneakers complete the outfit, if you can call it that when all I did was reach into my closet and yank out the first things I could find.

At only eight in the morning, most of the campers in Oak Crest seem to be still asleep. Or at least still in their campers. The spots are mainly *for* temporary residents, and only a few tent-ready areas remain nearer to the entrance to the campground, but even those are normally filled with truck-mounted campers and RVs instead. As I walk, the smell of campfires, a permanent fixture here, trickles into my nostrils, as does the scent of breakfast cooking that wafts from the few places I can see movement.

It's mostly only the people who love to fish that are awake right now, given that early-morning fishing is generally considered superior for those who want to catch something good, like largemouth bass.

I pass the bear tree and barely give it a glance, instead veering to the right to follow the road that takes me past a row of campers that are so close to one another that I could stand between them and touch one on each side if I stuck my arms out. These have been here forever, it seems. They're older models, and the decks built onto them look almost like a part of nature themselves.

The door of the third one opens, and Benjamin waves at me as he steps out and closes the door behind him, causing the lights hanging on the awning to jiggle.

"Good morning," he greets, going to the grill and flipping it up. I've never seen someone more in love with grilling than him, and I have to wonder if this is the only chance he gets to use one.

"Good morning, Ben," I reply, waving a hand at him. Neither dog approaches him, though I know they don't dislike the man. Vulcan just isn't that social, and Argus is normally stuck to me like glue.

"I'll be down to the House in an hour or so," he says as I pass, and I nod at his words. *I* certainly don't care when he gets there. I work at the House, or the camp store, in the morning most days, but he'll be doing business with Pat and Sam instead of me, I'm sure. They normally handle the long-time regulars like Ben's family and Carter.

The House itself is in sight, and from this side, its nickname is rather appropriate. The building *looks* like it could be a house, with its arched roof and windows. It's only the lattice-work fence and two bathroom entrances on this side that give it away as something else. A backdoor sits behind the bathrooms as well, and a large white box outside of it holds fishing crickets that I *know* must be chirping up a storm this early.

I don't take the backdoor however. I go around the side, the scent of chlorine from the pool down the hill to my left hitting me hard in the face. It'll be open by nine when the lifeguard gets here, though for now, the gate of the chain-link fence is padlocked to prevent anyone who doesn't want to try too hard from getting in.

The front of the House is just as homey as the sides. Large

windows show the shelves of supplies inside, and the area with the door is the one thing that, in my opinion, is out of place. The whole thing is thick glass, door included and arches up with the roof. The other side goes back to the vinyl, cream siding that matches the brown roof, and another cheery window sits on that wall as well.

I open the door and whistle, drawing Vulcan away from the deck sitting across the front of the store. He comes instantly, walking inside along with Argus as I follow and let the heavy door *whoosh* close behind me.

The fact that the owners are so open to me having both dogs here means that I'll probably never, *ever* leave this place. They'd practically insisted I have them and seemed more than a little reassured when I brought Vulc and Argus to the interview.

Well, if you could *call* it an interview. They'd hired me on the spot and had shown me the cabin that I'd moved into not much later.

As the door closes behind me, Sam looks up from the counter where the register sits, her worn face brightening into a wide smile. "Good morning, Sloane," she greets, voice gentle and containing an underlying musical note. I always wonder if she *did* sing in a past life or if she's just that thrilled with life all the time.

"Good morning," I greet, watching as Vulcan walks straight over and plants himself down beside his second-favorite person in the world.

Sam sets down the mail she'd been going through and turns her full attention on my dog, kneeling down in front of him so she can tell him what a good boy he is and give him all the attention he *clearly* never gets from me.

"I'm going to have to leave you alone for an hour or so," she tells me, standing once again with a grunt of pain. Her knees aren't great, I know, and I'm glad that Pat got her a new, tricked out golf cart to ride around the campground at the end of last year. It's done wonders for her arthritis, and she has a fun, musical horn to beep at everyone she comes across.

"That's fine." I snag a bottle of water and walk to the counter to go behind it as well. Argus comes with me as Vulcan goes to find the bed that's been put back here for both of the dogs to sleep on while I'm working. "Is something going on?"

"Oh, no. Nothing bad. But you know, two-fourteen had that storm damage last year," she reminds me, naming one of the permanently installed campers closer to the lake that had been hit when we'd had what I liked to call a *typhoon* at the end of last year's season. "They're finally having someone come out and finish fixing it. I'd like to go down there to make sure everything's all right, and they don't need any help."

Sam is absolutely the nicest person I've ever met. She tries to help as many people as she can, *whenever* she can, to the point that she should charge for her assistance, in my opinion. Her husband, Pat, is a lot like her. He's quieter, though. And that makes him come off as not quite so nice. Couple that with a heavy southern accent from his upbringing in Appalachia, and it means that a lot of people don't know how to read the taciturn older man.

"Oh, right. Right." I search my brain, trying to remember just what kind of damage had been done to two-fourteen, but honestly, I can't remember. Roof damage, maybe? That was pretty common in storms. Or maybe a wrecked deck? "Is anyone checking in that I should expect?"

"Maybe." She frowns thoughtfully. "I got a call right before closing last night about a guy wanting to rent that last available cabin on the ridge." She gestures towards the lake and the cabins beyond the boat launch that sits at the end of our little cove. "But I don't know if he was serious."

"Okay. Well, it's still open. So I'll just let it go first come first serve?" I ask, and Sam nods her agreement and goes out from behind the counter, grabbing her light jacket from the hanger behind it.

"Once I'm back, we'll figure out lunch," Sam adds, going to the door. "Since Raven will be here too by then." Raven, the lifeguard, doesn't live near here but enjoys working at the campground too much to quit. The woman, who's in her late thirties, had taken it upon herself to make sure I had *self-saving skills* when it came to swimming. Even though actually being *in* the water isn't my favorite thing. I'm grateful, sure, but I'm not sure how necessary it was, given that I do not plan on plunging into the middle of the lake to save anyone anytime soon. Or getting stranded out there myself without a boat, paddle, or floaties.

Then again, I guess you never know.

The door closes behind her, and I set the mail to the side before checking the register and eyeing the store itself. We're due for another shipment of things. Specifically *s'mores things*, but we're still pretty well stocked, given how busy we are out of the high season.

Minutes later, the door opens, prompting me to glance up to see someone I don't recognize. The woman smiles apologetically, as if she's somehow bothering me, and comes to the counter to place her hands on it gingerly. "Could you tell me how to get to the Colidale Marina?" she asks softly, voice barely above a whisper.

I blink and give her my best customer service smile as I rest my hands on the counter and splay my fingers. "Oh, sure. That's no problem. So you're going to leave the normal way." I gesture to the hill that dips down just outside the House and then goes back up across from us, the narrow road winding up towards the highway. "Then take a right. Once you hit Arkala's small excuse for a downtown, about five miles or so from here, you'll start seeing signs for it. You make a right at the first light, follow that road, and it's about four miles that way, then you'll take another right."

"Okay. Do you know if they have anything available today?" She pulls her hands back and looks around, eyes landing on the t-shirts hanging on the wall that each feature OAK CREST CAMPGROUND in big letters somewhere on the fabric.

"I don't, unfortunately," I say. "We're not affiliated with them at all. But uh…" I lean forward and twist to look at the rack of pamphlets that sits on the counter, just behind the magnets that *also* say the name of the campground. "Here you go. Their number is on here, and directions, in case I wasn't great at being clear." I was, and it's not difficult to get there, but I've learned not to underestimate how easily people will fuck up when they're driving somewhere.

The blonde woman takes the pamphlet with a smile and covers her mouth as she yawns. "Okay. Thank you. I really appreciate it." Without buying anything, she goes back to the door, exiting without another word.

"You're welcome," I tell the empty air, ducking down to grab the almost-empty bowl of water from behind the counter. With it in hand, I go to the back room, where the small break area is, and rinse it out before letting the water run into it to refill the bowl.

The door opens as I do, naturally, and I call above the water, "just a second!" So that they know the shop is not, in fact, abandoned and that I'm coming back in a second.

Moments later, I flip the water off and pick up the nearly-full bowl as I walk back into the main area of the shop. "Sorry about that," I say, catching a glimpse of a man gazing up at the wall of pictures featuring people who caught something impressive in the lake and had come back here to get their photos taken. Some of the photos are old and worn at this point, and I'm internally cringing as I wait for the day someone touches one, and it instantly turns to dust.

I go behind the counter and pause, my eyes on the dog bed where only Argus lays, tail thumping on the ground.

Where the heck is Vulcan?

Setting the bowl down, I turn to look behind me, my eyes instantly finding and zeroing in on my ferocious, anti-social guard dog.

Who, currently is sitting next to the man and bathing his hand with licks as his other hand rubs at his ears.

"Umm." I stare at them, my brain taking a minute to process that. It's cute...in a really weird way, like something out of a rom-com that I'd fall asleep twenty minutes into.

Then the man looks up, and *he* looks like something straight out of a dark romance-slash-erotica movie that I'd only be able to find online or behind a paywall.

"Is it okay if I pet him?" he asks, his voice soft and a bit higher than I'm expecting. He looks like someone who could *growl* with ease, as weird as that sounds, so to hear him sound melodic and friendly seems...off.

Then again, who am I to say? I've never met him before, obviously. And all I can do is stand here and stare at his dark, curly hair that's cut longer on top than on the sides and wonder how in the world this man has better lashes than most women I've met.

"Uh. Sure?" I say, shrugging one shoulder. "He's normally not so friendly. I'm surprised, I guess, that he's all over you like that."

His smile widens. "Maybe he's just a really excellent judge of people, and he likes me?" he chuckles, hazel eyes glittering with amusement.

"Sure." Frankly, Vulcan doesn't even *like* people most of the time unless they've fed him. And only then when they've given him something *really* tasty, like chicken. Sam, as sweet as she is, had to win him over that way as well, back when I'd first started.

So for him to just walk up to this guy is a surprise.

"I called last night." The man straightens and walks to the counter, accompanied by Vulcan, who moves to sit on his foot when he stops across on the other side of the raised, flat surface. He glances down again, smiles, and gives Vulcan back his hand so the German Shepherd can mouth it affectionately.

How fucking weird. If I didn't know better, I'd say he'd met my dog before. But I've certainly never seen this guy in my life.

"And I absolutely should've booked the cabin the owners said was available, but I wasn't sure," he admits with a small, almost apologetic shrug. "I just wasn't sure it was what I wanted."

"But you're sure today?" I ask, wondering what could've changed overnight.

He nods once, his eyes finding and holding mine. "I'm absolutely sure," he promises. "This is like, the hidden gem of Colidale Lake, you know?"

"It's a pretty nice campground," I agree. "And you're in luck since no one has come in to rent that cabin yet."

"Probably the luckiest I've been in a month," the man chuckles. "I have my boat with me as well. Is a dock slip extra?"

"No, it's included," I tell him, fighting the urge to crane my neck to see what kind of boat he has. Sometimes I'm surprised by what people bring here, though not that often. Most of the time, it's just fishing boats, speedboats, jet skis, and the odd pontoon here and there, which *would* require a bigger spot. "What kind of boat?"

"Speedboat. A normal spot will do," he tells me like he's

had this conversation a thousand times before. And maybe he has.

"Perfect." On the computer I bring up the rental page for the last cabin and reach behind me to grab the little rubber keychain that's attached to a key for the dock. "So you're going to be in cabin six. It's the furthest one over there." I point out the glass of the front wall and glance up to see he's staring at *me* instead of looking where I'm pointing.

A soft, teasing smile flits across his lips, and I narrow my eyes in confusion and bemusement. "It's that way," I tell him again, in case he's *confused*.

"Your eyes are two different colors." The words come out as delighted. Like this is some added bonus he hadn't expected.

"Uh, yeah," I reply, blinking at him in mild surprise. It's generally something people comment on, but they don't normally look so *excited* like it does something personally for *them*. "It's called–"

"Heterochromia," he breaks in, then frowns. "Sorry. I shouldn't have interrupted you. It's really pretty."

"Normally, people think it's weird since this eye is so much lighter," I admit, tapping just under my blue eye.

"It's not weird," he assures me, still looking thrilled. "Anyway, I'm sorry. Go on telling me about the cabin, please?"

"It's at the end of that row over there." This time, he obediently looks to where I'm pointing. "Watch out for the hill that comes around. I *know* it's steep as heck. It's technically a family cabin, so there's a kitchen and living area on the first floor, along with two bedrooms and a bathroom. Up top is a loft with two twin beds."

"Then I'll clearly have to sleep somewhere new every night," the man chuckles and turns back to look at me again. "To see which bed is the best."

It's not the answer I'm expecting and draws a soft huff of

laughter from me as my mouth turns up into a half-smile. "How long are you staying?"

"Oh, hmm." He rocks back on his heels, hands coming to rest on the counter, and when I look down, I'm surprised to see that the knuckles of his left hand are tattooed, along with the back of his hand, and it continues under the sleeve of his jacket.

I wonder how far up it goes.

"Let's do...ten days? My friends are telling me I *really* need a vacation, so I guess I'm going to trust them this time."

"Okay." It doesn't affect me either way, and I put that on the page I have pulled up. I certainly won't mind looking at him for *ten* whole days. "What's your name?"

"Virgil Olsen," he tells me smoothly. "What's yours?"

Is he flirting with me? I can't help but glance at him, and his eyes on mine, coupled with his soft smile, make my stomach twist with something like anticipation.

Down girl, I tell myself. *He's just being a tease. You don't even know him. He could be weird or something. Well, weirder than you.*

"It's Sloane," I reply. "Payment method?"

Out of his wallet, he produces a credit card that lands on the counter with a flourish. I type in the numbers, occasionally glancing at him as he stares out the window at what he can see of the campground.

"How old are you?" I ask, keeping my voice businesslike. I don't *need* to ask or anything. We rent to anyone over twenty-one, and he's got to be older than that by a couple of years, at least. Though his sharply handsome face and full mouth are throwing me off.

His eyes find mine and narrow slightly, like he's about to call me out on my question and why I'm asking.

"I just turned thirty," Virgil replies after a moment's consideration. "Why? If I tell you my birthday is today, do I get a discount? Will you jump up on this counter and sing to me?"

"No," I snort. "I absolutely will not." I type on the keyboard again like I *did* need to know his age for something, then slide his card back to him.

Before I can move my hand, his tattooed, tanned fingers come down over mine, holding me there for a second.

"Thanks, Sloane," he says, his voice just a little bit deeper and a little bit darker when he says it.

He's fucking with me.

It's obvious that he is, and I look up at him with my lips pressed together to assess his expression.

Though what I find is only a polite, friendly smile and an almost-blank expression. Like he's just some pleasant, empty-headed animatronic running through the motions.

If anything, it's kind of creepy.

I extract my hand from his and grab the key from under the counter, making sure it's the right one as I lay it on the counter as well. "Is one key okay?" I ask, glancing up at him once more.

"Sure," he says. "It's just me, anyway. Do you need anything else?"

I shake my head and push the dock key towards him again as well. "The cabin should be fully stocked with essentials, but if not, you can come back down or call," I offer. "And one of us can bring stuff up to you. Vulcan?" At his name, the dog leaves Virgil's foot and comes back around to slip behind the counter, leaning on my leg and panting up at me.

"Your dogs are adorable," he tells me and pockets his card. "See you later, Sloane." It's weird how he says my name, like he *enjoys* saying it. Or like he knows me.

I don't get it.

"Have a nice stay. And uh, I hope you like the cabin," I reply, watching him until he's out of the building entirely.

When he's gone, I turn and scowl at Vulcan, hand going to my hip. "What the hell?" I ask him, cupping his muzzle playfully. "Why do you like him so much, huh?"

Of course, the mostly black Shepherd doesn't answer, but he does turn his head so he can put my hand in his mouth and get his slobber all over it.

4

By the time Raven's checked in and then gone back to the pool, still with no sign of Sam coming back, I'm bored. Working in the House is probably my least favorite part of the job, and there's not much I can do to make it more interesting except scroll through my newsfeed on my phone or look through the relationship-advice side of social media so I can cringe at people's lousy life situations that I don't envy at all.

I'm also starting to wonder if Sam has encountered some kind of issue at two-fourteen. Pat hasn't come in, meaning he might be there as well, and I sit back on my stool as I glance for the fortieth time out the window, my eyes drifting to cabin six that still looks *exactly* the same as it had a while ago.

The first thing Virgil does is get his boat in the water. A process I'd headed outside to watch, telling myself it was only to look at what kind of boat he'd brought to the lake. And he hadn't surprised me...entirely. The speedboat was shiny and sparkled red in the dim light, its white interior spotless and the silver rails around the edges gleaming. With the ease of long practice, he'd backed it off the trailer, something I'd seen go wrong *many* times before and had guided it over to his spot before walking back out and going to his truck to take the trailer to where the others were stored.

For some reason, he'd looked back up at the front of the House, and when he'd seen me there, he'd grinned and waved, making me grit my teeth and wave back, my insides squirming with the humiliation of being caught.

He'd gone to the cabin, presumably, but that meant I couldn't see him anymore. The only door to it was facing my side of the cove, technically, but it was more than a hundred yards away, and there was every chance that he'd gone in with his stuff, come back out, and taken off. Or that he was wandering the campground or on his boat.

And I'm sure as hell not about to start stalking him to find out.

The phone rings, and I pick it up to answer easily, "Oak Crest Campground, how can I help you?"

Only to get faced with no reply. I blink, gaze up at the ceiling, and wait a few seconds for the line to clear in case the person is driving anywhere nearby. The service here *sucks*, and this kind of thing is common, especially if someone is driving in and needs to get ahold of us. "Hello?" I try again after a few moments.

But there's still no response.

"I think we have a bad connection," I go on, leaning my hip against the counter and looking at the wall with one arm folded across my stomach. "Maybe you can try calling me back–"

A soft exhale meets my ears, almost too soft for me to hear. Something shifts in the background, and I freeze.

What in the world?

"Hello?" I try again, my words less friendly this time and

colder. A glance at the screen of the phone shows an *unknown number*, but that's not uncommon when people call from a private line. "Can you hear me–" The line goes dead while I'm speaking, and I pull it away again to stare at the phone in absolute confusion. "Okay," I mutter, crossing my ankles. "That was really fucking weird, huh guys?" The two dogs look up from the bed where they're dozing, and Argus thumps his tail in response to my words.

The phone rings again, making me jump a little as the screen lights up above my fingers. I check again, and when I see the *unknown caller* flashing across the screen, I genuinely consider not answering it.

But I'm clearly a sucker for punishment, so I sigh and hit the green button before bringing it to my ear with a slightly grumpy, "Hello? Thanks for calling Oak Crest Campground. How can I help you?"

I'm fully expecting another lack of response.

I'm *not* expecting the gravelly male smoker's voice that says, with some surprise, "*Sloane?*"

My hand tightens around the phone until the plastic creaks. I *know* this unknown caller, and I hate that fact with every fiber of my being.

"How did you get this number?" I ask through numb lips.

"*Sloane, I've been trying to call you for weeks. Kate says you have my number blocked just like your mom does, so I had to figure out how to get ahold of you this way, instead. Couldn't believe you're working at a campground.*" The man chuckles ruefully. "*You never exactly liked the outdoors much–*"

"*Aunt Kate* told you where I'm working?" It takes a moment to realize that my mom probably told her ex-sister-in-law in passing, and when my stepfather had gotten out of prison last month, my aunt had probably run to tell her brother whatever he'd asked when he came calling.

What a *bitch*.

"*Of course she did. We're family, and I've been trying to talk to you—*"

"I don't want to talk to *you*." The anger in my voice surprises me, as does the cold hate that creeps up my fingers and snakes through my veins. Argus is off the bed in an instant, a paw on my leg as he whines and pushes his nose under my hand that's balled in my hoodie.

"*I get that you're upset. But please, I really want to talk. Things are different now. The doctors at the prison—*"

"No," I say the word as forcefully as I can without yelling. "I don't want to talk to *you*." The scar above my sternum seems to burn, even though it's long healed. "Don't you ever call this number again. And don't try to contact me *ever* again. Mom and I are done with you, *Anthony*." While I'd once referred to him as Dad a very long time ago, those days were long gone. They'd *been* gone ever since he'd gotten high, kidnapped me, and almost *killed* me.

So why the hell did they let him out of prison? Mom knew, obviously. She'd told me they'd let him out on some kind of parole and had given me his number to block after he'd called her. But that was supposed to be the end of it. He didn't know me anymore. He didn't know where I work, or anything like that. Hell, for all he supposedly knew, I was still in Columbus.

But apparently, his sister just couldn't let things die.

I suck in a breath and hang up suddenly, just as he starts talking once more. I don't care what he has to say. Whether it's an apology, a promise, or a threat. They're all the same to me, and I don't have time for it or the mental capacity to deal with it.

Not when just his voice has my heart racing and my brain trying to set me back about ten steps. As I lay the phone down,

Argus jumps up to press against my chest, licking my face as he whines and tries to distract me.

"Thank you, Argus," I breathe, setting the phone back in its cradle much more gently than I want to. I suck in a breath, then another, my head spinning and feeling like I can't get enough oxygen.

I need to go outside.

Moving out from behind the counter, I whistle to get Vulcan's attention and stride for the glass door, barely slowing down as I open it and keep walking with the dogs onto the pavement near me. I can't *leave* the House while I'm the only one working, but I can walk a little.

At least to the deck on the other side of the wide pavement drive that perches over the path that leads to the lake.

My steps on the wood make it creak, and I go straight to the edge and get on my knees on the bench that encircles the whole deck and place my hands on the flat wood railing. I suck in a much longer breath, feeling slightly better now that I'm outside, and rest my head on my arms as I focus just on breathing and nothing else.

I'm *fine*. I'm mostly, probably fine. I just need to chill out because *freaking out* isn't conducive to getting through the day.

But I also need to call Mom.

Beside me, I can still feel Argus as attentive as ever, and I know that if I turn over and sit on the bench properly, he'll be in my lap and across my legs to try to ground me. But I'm not going to freak out. I'm going to suck in a few more deep breaths and *not*–

"Are you okay?" The warm, honeyed voice makes me whirl around, and I nearly lose my balance on the deck.

Behind me, Virgil stands against the far rail, hands in the pockets of his black jeans as he watches me with narrowed eyes under heavy, long lashes.

Of *course,* he's here to watch me nearly fall apart.

"What?" I ask as if I hadn't heard him. I had, and that's the problem. I'm not sure how to answer just yet.

"You nearly hit me with the door when you came out," he says, offering me a soft smile. "I was worried you were having some kind of emergency." Vulcan sits at his side, wagging his tail, and absently Virgil reaches out to stroke his ears again.

I can't help but, again, wonder why my dog has taken to him like a long-lost owner, but I push it from my mind and attempt to smile.

Though I promptly fail, and I don't try again.

"I just...yeah. I'm good." I clear my throat and busy myself by taking my hair down from its ponytail to let it fall around my shoulders. Combing it out with my fingers, I take a breath, wondering if I can make as much noise as possible and he'll just *go away.*

Obviously, I don't want company right now. Doesn't he see that?

"You sure?"

"Yeah, I'm absolutely sure." I flash him a false, bright smile and wind my auburn hair back up into a bun. I love having it long, but there's no way in hell I could work here and let it fall all the way to the middle of my back during the day. I'd die of heatstroke, for one. "Sorry for umm. Almost hitting you with the door?" I ask to make sure I heard him right. I hadn't *seen* him when I'd come out of the House, but that's not saying much, seeing as I'm pretty upset.

"It's okay. I might've caught it if my face was really in danger. My friends all say that I care about my face *too much* and that I develop superhuman reflexes when it's in danger." His teasing lilt gives me pause, and I look at him with a question on my face.

"Really?" I can't help but ask. "That seems...dramatic?"

"*I'm* dramatic if you haven't noticed," he assures me, putting a hand on his chest. For the first time, I notice he looks a little...ruffled. Like he did something strenuous or rolled around in a bed before he got back here...though I choose to cut that thought off *right there* instead of letting it go any further. "What do you need, anyway?"

"S'mores stuff," he says, shoving his hands in his pockets and giving me a boyish grin. "Look, I'm kind of addicted, and I'm a sugar fiend. Was this vacation an elaborate excuse to make s'mores? Maybe. And you'll break my heart if you tell me you're out in the store."

"I don't think we're out," I assure him, walking past him and going back towards the building. He shifts subtly, giving me *just* enough room to walk, but I don't say a word as I brush his arm accidentally.

How far do those tattoos go? I can't help but wonder again. "You coming?" I ask when he doesn't move, and I've nearly reached the door.

Virgil turns to watch me, his eyes narrowed, and when he opens his mouth to say something, he closes it before replying, "Yeah, sorry. Your dog just doesn't want me to go anywhere." It's true, and it takes him a moment to get Vulcan to move so that he *can* follow me back into the store for his marshmallows, graham crackers, and chocolate that he buys the last of.

"I'll be back for more," he tells me, brandishing the plastic bag as he turns to leave. "So make sure you get some back in stock, okay?"

"You could just go to the store," I point out with a snort as he heads towards the door. "You know, the *real* store?"

He doesn't reply verbally but shakes his head and pushes out of the building again, plastic bag swinging at his side.

5

That night, I again fall asleep on the sofa, the TV on to help me forget the day. It's easier this way when I can keep the TV on and just loud enough to distract me from my stepdad's call. I haven't gotten around to calling Mom yet, though I want to. I need to, but I don't know what to say. I don't want to drag *her* back into this either, and I know she'll insist on coming up from Columbus or having me move back home with her.

But I don't want to move home. I've had enough of living there, being treated like I'm fragile, and feeling like I can barely take care of myself. Maybe living in a campground isn't amazing or the epitome of what I *should* be doing at twenty-seven, but it works for me.

And I like it here.

God, I just hope my stepfather doesn't try to take that away. Or worse, succeed in doing so.

It feels like I've just drifted off when a cold nose pushes against my hand. I moan in my sleep, barely conscious, and flip over on the sofa to face the other way.

This time, Vulcan finds my shoulder. He whines softly, and finally I sit up to glare at my dark Shepherd that stands next to the sofa with his tail wagging hopefully.

"Are you joking?" I mumble quietly, hearing Argus *snoring* from the other room. "Like, you have to be joking, right?"

Unfortunately, he does not seem to be joking. I stumble to my feet and stare at the television, trying to get my bearings and *wake up* before going outside. Yet again, I would rather be *asleep*. But also, I'm glad to get the chance to change out of my denim shorts and into my softer sleep shorts.

"Please don't go off into the woods," I beg, going towards the door and opening it. I flip on the light with my other hand, squinting and trying not to look at the porch lamp that, even in its dim state, is too much for my sleep-addled brain.

Predictably, Vulcan walks behind the cabin, going towards the firepit and the picnic table beyond. This time, however, my shoes are by the door, and I put them on, just in case he doesn't come back in about twenty seconds. There's no way he has to do more than *pee* at…I grab my phone off the end table near the door where I'd chucked it and sigh. *Three thirty-two in the morning.* I'm going to be up in four hours, and while I would rather be awake now than thirty minutes before I need to get up, I'd still rather be *asleep*.

It takes me a few more seconds to realize Vulcan isn't back, and I can't hear him.

"God, I'm going to have to put you on a leash," I mutter to myself, wondering if I still have the long, thirty-foot leash that I used to train him. He's never done this to me before. Normally he's in and out when he has to go at night, and it hasn't been multiple nights in a row in a *long* time.

Why is he being so weird now?

"Vulc?" I call, hoping that he'll come running back around the cabin.

He doesn't.

A small amount of fear climbs through my body, digging icy claws into my insides as I step out onto the porch and flip on the fairy lights. "Vulcan!" I call louder this time, and walk around towards the firepit.

He's not there. Nor is he in the surrounding trees that I can see. It's not like him to run off. He's taciturn, unfriendly, and doesn't have enough of a prey drive that I've ever actually worried about him running off. Not since he was a lot younger, anyway.

My shoes scuff on the gravel, and I take a moment to be glad that I kept my shoes by the door *just in case*. I had hoped that Vulcan wouldn't want to go outside again, but I'd been wrong.

When I get to the edge of the woods, I stop, gazing into the absolute pitch black of the trees that the light from the cabin barely illuminates. A few feet in, everything goes pitch black, and I can barely see more than the first few rows of trees clearly.

I can't help it. My hands clench at my sides, and my heart pounds a few warning beats in my throat as the sound of crickets and frogs becomes oppressive in the air around me.

I'm afraid of the dark. Not always, but right now, standing here alone, I can't help the swell of fear in my chest or the way the blackness bends and creeps around me.

"Vulcan!" I call, trying to keep my voice steady. "Come here!"

I'm grateful when I hear the sound of paws crashing through the brush, and within moments I see my dog, all happy tail wagging and pricked ears, coming towards me unharmed.

"You've got to stop going so far," I tell him, power-walking back towards the cabin.

He looks up at the sound of my voice, mouth moving like he's chewing something. *Again.*

"Did you get into something?" I pause, now safely back in the light from the porch, and kneel in front of him, his muzzle in my hand. It takes a few seconds to pry it open, and I'm half-convinced I'm going to find the remains of a squirrel or some other small animal.

But instead, there's nothing. Except, when Vulcan heavily exhales a puff of warm air, the smell of *peanut butter* hits my nose, and I frown.

"What the *fuck?*" I mumble, getting to my feet. "How did you get into *peanut butter?*" I suppose it's not *impossible* that someone lost a jar, and it ended up all the way back here. Storms and the wind are a bitch, after all. But it's still just so... weird, I guess.

Back inside, Vulcan goes right back to my room and hops onto my bed, twisting in a circle a couple of times before he flops to the mattress and lets out a huge doggy sigh.

"Well, sorry, your majesty," I tell him, grabbing my pj's from the end of the bed. I strip quickly and take a moment to stretch when I'm fully nude.

This time, when my eyes catch the window and the trees beyond, however, I pause and frown.

Why do I keep seeing something in the trees? The question is an unwelcome one, and I pull my t-shirt on before going to stand at the window. Even if there was someone out there, the window is at hip-level for me, so I'm covered enough to look around at the black woods beyond my cabin.

There's really...nothing there. If anything, it's probably the glare from my bedroom light, and being jumpy from my stepdad calling is just making things worse.

But you weren't jumpy last night, my brain supplies unhelpfully before I silence that train of thought. I pull on my shorts and go to the light, turning it off before falling into bed with the dogs.

Thankfully, there are neither snores nor pants tonight. Yet.

"Can we stop doing this, Vulc?" I moan, dragging the sheet up over me. "I'm getting tired of running after you in the dark, okay?"

In answer, the German shepherd throws himself across my feet and *sighs* with the force of a tornado.

When the storm rumbles through around noon, I know that it's going to be a problem. Thankfully, I'm up in the House, not wandering the campground, and I get to watch from the windowed lounge beside the store itself as Raven closes up the pool and jogs into the House as well.

"Holy *shit*," she whistles, coming to sit on the sofa beside me. "That's some storm we've got rolling in."

"Hell yeah," I agree, patting the sofa beside me so that Argus jumps up to lounge across my lap. "There's going to be some damage, I bet. The wind is insane."

"Probably two-fourteen again. They *just* got that roof on yesterday," the lifeguard sighs, leaning against the sofa back.

"It's *always* two-fourteen," I grump, knowing that it's unfair to call out one of the oldest units on the site. My eyes flick back to the windows, and I watch as campers scurry around, trying to secure their awnings, tents, or other outdoor belongings. The front door opens, but neither of us move. Sam is in the store, and both of us *are* technically on break. If it's someone who needs something and isn't just looking for a quick bit of shelter from the rain, they can go to her.

Sure enough, low voices sound from the counter, and I recognize Carter's stilted speech as he says something, and Sam laughs her reply.

"I'm going to go outside and listen," I say, getting to my

feet as the rain starts to pound against the glass. "If you need me, I guess...don't?" I give Raven a quick grin as she flips me off, rolling her eyes as she fights her own smile.

"Whatever," the lifeguard says. "You want to do dinner tonight?"

"I guess. Huckleberry is open today," I say, naming one of the few cafés in the area with an amazing reputation but terribly sporadic hours. "If you want some pancakes."

"I *really* want some pancakes," Raven assures me, pulling her long red hair into a ponytail that's lower and messier than mine. "I'm off at six."

"I'm never off." We trade a last quick grin, and Raven snorts out a laugh as I walk back into the main part of the store, where Carter stands at the counter as Sam counts out change.

"Hey Carter," I greet, lifting my hand to greet the older fisherman. He barely turns, and when he does, he gives me a quick, disapproving once over.

Carter has never seemed to *really* like me, though I'm not quite sure why. Because I exist? Because I wear mostly black? Maybe I *breathe* too loudly in his presence.

"Pretty bad storm, huh?" he grunts after a few moments. He reaches his hands out for the dogs, and I let Argus know he's free to go before the Shepherd will approach Carter, sniffing hands that have more than once given him strips of fresh fish.

"I bet two-fourteen takes a hit," I say in agreement.

"Shhh," Sam frowns and shakes her head, though there's amusement in her gray eyes. "From your mouth to God's ears, Sloane. I don't want to have to patch that roof *again* while they wait for insurance."

"They need a new camper entirely," Carter grumbles, taking the change and his slushie. He's the only person, other than me that I know of who partakes of the blue slushies we sell for *some* unfathomable reason in the camp store.

"*Thank* you," I agree, going to the slushie machine and pouring myself one as well. "Are you heading out in this, Carter?"

"I'm parked right there," he mutters, jerking his chin towards the front of the building. I glance around and see his old green truck parked there, along with a large, sleek black truck behind it.

I do a double-take and then glance around the store. There's no one here other than Raven and us, and none of us drives a truck like that.

Weird. The front of the building isn't exactly *for* long-term parking, though I'm sure Sam and Pat will forgive someone for waiting out the rain here.

"I'm going out back with the crickets," I say, whistling for both dogs to show them where we're going.

"Hey, Sloane?" Pat's voice from the office stops me in my tracks, and I poke my head in before I leave the building entirely. Thunder rumbles, shaking the House, and as I watch, he lays some papers to the side. "Why don't you do a big walk-through tomorrow after all this shit blows through?" His accent is thick and makes his words hard to understand. It sounds like he's chewing on them, the same way he chews the tobacco that sits against his lower lip. "It's supposed to storm all night, and I'd like to know about any damage early. Is that all right?"

"Yeah, no problem," I assure him. "Want me to check Highland and Lake Place too?" While the two residential streets that border one side of the campground aren't *ours*, we face issues when they do. It's better to know when they're going to need work done, in case we need to *not* book out the places closest to there.

Weird how campers don't enjoy the sound of construction equipment repairing roads or roofs at four a.m.

"If you please," Pat grunts, adjusting his glasses. "Thanks again."

"No problem." I give him a half-salute that he pointedly ignores and turn to leave, going out the back door while still remaining in the safety of the covered outdoor hallway with the crickets and the entrance to the ladies' bathroom.

The storm has picked up by the time I let the door close behind me, and when I peek out from under the awning where rain runs in *rivers* from the gutters, the sky is nearly black with the storm.

"You aren't going out in this, are you?" a familiar, honeyed voice hums from my right. I jump, a small sound leaving me that I will not admit to being a squeak, and turn to see that *Virgil* is sitting against the stone wall beside the large container that holds the crickets. His knees are half-up, showing off his long legs, and he wears the same black jacket he'd worn yesterday.

Again, my eyes are drawn to the tattoos on his knuckles, and when my eyes reach his face, I find his gaze already on mine. As if he'd been *waiting* for me to look at him.

Vulcan wanders over instantly and sits down beside him, bathing his hands in affectionate licks.

"What? No. *God,* no," I assure him. "I'm just here to watch the storm." It's weird that he's out here too, but I drag over a plastic chair close enough to the edge of the overhang that I can see part of the sky, but not close enough to get more than occasionally sprinkled with water.

Argus lays at my feet, having no urge to join his friend in showing affection to the camper.

Absently, Virgil's hand goes to Vulcan's ears, and I marvel

again at how Vulcan's affection for the man seems to have doubled overnight.

Maybe he's just a dog person? Since animals can supposedly sense that kind of thing, I suppose I shouldn't be surprised.

"I like storms," he admits. "Sometimes. But not when I'd planned on going out on the lake." He gives me a quick, wry smile that doesn't reach his eyes as I watch him.

"Why are you back here?" I ask finally. "Is that your truck out front?" I've seen his truck before, sure. But jumping to conclusions seems *rude*.

"That's my truck," he assures me. "And I'm back *here* because I don't feel like going out in the rain."

"But if you get in your truck, that's like twenty steps *max* in the rain," I point out.

"The *torrential downpour*, you mean."

"Sure, yeah. Anyway. Twenty steps, then maybe five more when you get to the cabin before you're covered by the roof of the deck. And you could be back in your cabin in minutes. And you'd only spend what? Twenty-five steps in the rain?" I raise my brows, still not understanding why he's *here,* of all places.

"You seem really sure of that number," Virgil replies after a minute or so. "Want to go with me to see if you're right? My legs are longer than yours, so it may only take me twenty-one."

"What makes you think I haven't already counted?"

"Oh? To *my* cabin? Have you been there often?"

"I work here, don't I?" I hold his gaze with my own mismatched eyes until he looks away, a grin curling over his full lips.

"Adorable," he says at last, and I'm glad he's *not* looking at me because I can feel myself heat up, and I'm sure I'm turning red.

"So, why are you here?" I prompt, reminding him of my other question.

"Maybe I really needed crickets."

"Maybe you don't look anything like a fisherman who *does*." While he had me a little tongue-tied yesterday, that's worn off enough that I don't mind speaking my mind to him. It's not like he's more than a stranger to me, anyway. And in nine days, he'll pack up, leave, and I'll never see him again. There's no point or need in acting like something I'm not, even to get his attention.

"You're so *harsh*, Sloane." He looks up at me again, and when he does, there's something in his gaze that goads and dares me to go on. "Are you like this with all the boys who sit next to the crickets?"

The way he says it catches me off guard enough that I have to work to hide my grin, but when his eyes shine with triumph, I know that I've failed.

"Most of the boys around here *don't* sit with the crickets. And the ones that do never want to talk to me," I point out finally.

"Their loss. You're more charming than all the crickets in all the buckets in all the world." It's such a stupid, strange thing to say, and I don't know how to take it.

"You don't look like someone who goes camping a lot," I say finally, dragging a foot up to rest my heel on the plastic of the chair under me. "No offense."

"Some taken," he admits. "Why don't I look like a camper?"

I gesture at him, but he only stares at me and says, "Use your words for me, won't you, Sloane?"

A tremor goes down my spine when he says my name because it really shouldn't be that hot to hear it on his lips. It's unfair, quite frankly. And I'd like a refund.

"You're too *fancy* to go camping. You look like you paid too much for those jeans to get them dirty here. And your boat is way nicer than most people who come here."

"Well, I'm not exactly tent camping," he points out.

"Right, but you look like someone who owns a huge-ass house around here, not someone who comes here with his dad-vest and fishing gear, okay?" I don't know how to explain it better than that, and I frown at him. "You get what I mean?"

"I guess. But I'm a little offended by it. I *like* camping. One of my best friends is *really* attached to this campground north of Akron, actually. Camp Crystal Pond. He's even *named* after it, so we used to go there all the time." Virgil chuckles. "I probably have a lot more camping experience than you think I do. Even of the tent-variety."

"Uh-huh." It isn't that I don't believe him, and I'm absolutely going to look up Camp Crystal Pond later if I remember. Just to see if it exists.

He looks at me again from under his long lashes. "Careful with all that derision," he warns, his grin still friendly. "You might hurt my feelings."

"I'll try to spare them," I assure him.

"Good. If not, I'd have to put you in one of my articles, and I might not paint you in a very *flattering* light."

That catches me off guard, and I take a moment before asking, "What?"

"I'm a reporter." He leans his head back against the stone. "A crime reporter, normally. The *murder* kind."

"That's incredibly morbid."

"You have a problem with morbid?"

"No, no. Not at all. I like the *Hostel* movies just as much as the next gore-enthusiast," I assure him with complete honesty.

His smile seems to take him off guard, and he reaches up a hand to cover it until he can get control of himself again. "Which is your favorite?"

"Two, obviously. There's literally no other right answer."

"Fair. But I only like it because of the modern Lady Bathory scene."

It takes me a moment to remember, and I curl my nose in disgust. "Oh yeah? Are you taking notes on how to bathe in the blood of virgins to maintain your silky smooth skin?"

"I'm taking notes on how to build a bathtub big enough to do so," Virgil corrects. "Why do you like it?"

"Because the girl becomes the killer without much hesitation," I say quickly, not having to think about my answer. I find his gaze as I continue, the rain pounding on the roof above us with no sign of stopping. "When she's faced with dying or having to join them, she doesn't even try to be the better person. I really like that in someone who's trying to get out of a bad situation. Moral high ground is for the privileged, you know?"

"Does that mean you'd cut off a guy's junk and toss it to a dog if you needed to survive?" Virgil asks, eyes dancing.

"Well, obviously," I snort. "Why do you think I have two German Shepherds with me all the time?" It's a joke, but the way he looks at me makes me think that he takes it as something more, and I don't know how to respond except to chuckle at my own words like they were basically an empty promise anyway.

6

"I am *not* letting you out at three a.m. tonight," I say, staring into Vulcan's dark eyes as the dog pants happily. Both he and Argus are on the couch for once, and I don't plan on letting them into the bedroom for at least a little while. Not when they'll be all over the bed, and I want to *use* the bed for more than just sleeping.

Thunder rolls in the distance, signaling the arrival of another spring storm. It probably won't be as bad as the one earlier today, but it's not like I *mind* or anything.

"You've both gone out. You're fine. If you try me *one more time* this week, I'm pulling out your leash," I assure him. Behind him, on the other end of the couch, Argus thumps his tail like it's him I'm talking to instead of Vulcan.

Finally, I stand, knowing that my dogs have no idea what I'm talking about, and give them both a quick scratch on their noses. Argus goes to move, but I murmur a quick 'stay' and go back into my room, shutting the door behind me.

Somehow, instead of watching some stupid drama, or even a bloody, gross gore movie like I'd thought I would, I ended up sitting on my bed, laptop open and navigating back to one of my favorite porn videos. I hadn't *meant* to. Really, it just happened. But it's not like anyone else is here, and when I spent the last part of my night reading reverse harem by the fire outside, I guess I can't be too surprised that I want to do something other than *sleep*.

With all the lights off except for the one between my bed and the open window where only a screen separates me from the approaching storm, I fall back onto the bed with a sigh, my laptop beside me as I click play to finish the last of the video.

Again, I'm oh-so-grateful that my cabin is in the middle of nowhere, and I don't need to worry about not making any kind of noise. I shimmy out of my shorts and reach into the drawer beside the bed, stomach clenching as I tap the end of the small vibrator a few times to make sure it's charged.

I've learned the hard way that toys can and *will* die at the absolute worst time if you try to play fast and loose with them, so I avoid that whenever possible. There's nothing worse in the world than a vibrator dying *right* before an orgasm, I've come to learn. Literally *nothing worse*.

As the video ends, I close my laptop and shove it away, drawing my small vibrator down my body to tease at my clit. With my shorts off, I feel incredibly exposed, even though It's just me in my bedroom, and I shiver as I let my thighs fall to either side with a soft sigh.

Unfortunately, I'm not good at *teasing* myself. Within a few seconds, my vibrator is against my clit, and I circle it lightly, loving the almost-too-intense feeling of the vibration there. A soft sound leaves me, and I reach my other hand up to palm my breast, fingers teasing at my nipple.

This is when I wish I had a partner. At least a little bit. While I *love* my toys, and I know my own body extremely well, it's hard to keep doing more than one thing like I want to when it's just me here.

But I manage. My eyes slide closed as I run my vibrator up and down my slit, dipping it just inside my body and causing my stomach to twist in excitement before dragging it up to my clit again. I have a bigger toy, which I reach out and grab from the drawer, then place it under my pillow so that it's easier to reach, but I'm definitely going to take a few more minutes with just this one. Otherwise, this will be over way sooner than I want it to be since I don't know how to deny chasing my release as quickly as I can. Another thing I miss about having a partner.

I lift my t-shirt, exposing my breasts to the cool air of the cabin while the sounds from the woods fill my ears instead of the sound of what I've been watching. I *like* feeling vulnerable and exposed. I enjoy the way the air prickles my skin and how it feels almost dangerous to lie here with my legs spread like I'm inviting someone to join in.

Don't you dare, I tell my brain when it starts to conjure up *Virgil's* gorgeous face and what he might look like without his jacket. Is the idea of him pressing my thighs apart and kneeling between them, cock hard as he promises to fuck me a *very* enticing picture? Yeah. But I'm not sure it's what I want right now. At least not until he's checked out, and I don't have to see him during the day *and talk to him*.

"Fuck," I whisper, half-heartedly against my pillow as I circle my clit with my vibrator again. I open my eyes to look out the window, and this time I *refuse* to let my gaze find any sign of movement that'll ruin this for me.

Though, my phone ringing from the other room does just as good of a job.

I turn off the vibrator and groan loudly, not wanting to move from the bed. Surely this is *a joke*. My phone isn't *really* ringing. It's past midnight, so there's no way it's anything work-related.

Though it could be stepdad-related.

In the end, I decide to just not answer it. I can say I was asleep if it's something important, though I'm sure it's just spam.

The ringing stops, and I sigh, ready to go back to what I was doing.

Until it starts ringing *again*.

Sneering a few choice, four-letter words to myself, I yank my t-shirt back down over my breasts and get up, my vibrator joining the one under my pillow as I go to the door and pull it open. Both dogs are on the sofa still, and I can hear Argus's light snores while my phone continues to ring on the end table.

I shouldn't have left it in here. I hadn't *meant* to, either. But it sits on the end table across from the TV, the screen lighting up continuously as if to insult me.

In three strides, I'm across the room and answering the phone with an aggressively unhappy, "*What?*" Whether it's spam or my stepdad, this greeting is appropriate.

Instead, I get nothing. The only noises are the fan that I've had going for a few days now and the sound of thunder from outside. There's nothing, and when I look at the screen, I find that it says *Blocked Caller*.

"Anthony, is that you?" I snap, using my stepdad's name. "I swear to *fucking God,* if that's you, I'm going to flip out."

There's a sound like a whisper; then the phone goes dead.

Is that a confirmation that it was my stepdad? In my mind, it absolutely is. I feel vindicated and irritated, and when I look down, I find both dogs have their eyes on me, though Vulcan's ears are pricked like he's listening for something.

"You're not going out," I tell him. "At least not now." My happy feelings aren't *completely* ruined, and I'm going to salvage what I can of this, even if the end result is less than satisfying.

Quickly, I stomp back to my room, this time depositing my phone on the dresser by the door. My alarm is set for seven, and if it's there, then at least I'll have to physically get up to grab it. Plus, I'll still have to get up to let the dogs in, so if I need to, I'll grab it then. While I'm up, I move the laptop from the bed to the dresser closest to the door, and then I'm home-free. I fall onto the bed again and groan, eyes closed as I flex my fingers and try to shake the irritation out of my brain.

I'm going to make the best of this, damn it. I lift my hand, reaching for the vibrators that I'd put under my pillow. They're right where I'd left them, and I sigh as I grab my bullet once more, eyes closing as I turn it on and let my thighs fall open again. My free hand rucks up my t-shirt, and I roll my nipple between my fingers while I tease myself, absently looking towards the window.

Something's not quite right. The thought isn't enough to distract me. It's not enough to make me stop, but the longer I stare at the trees beyond the screen, the more I see that something's different.

The trees are clearer. They should be blurry behind the screen, but instead, they're *clear,* like the screen has completely vanished.

But that doesn't make any sense.

Suddenly something curls around my ankle, startling me, but when I jerk, I find I can't move. I look down, my stomach clenching, and as I watch, a white mask comes into view as the person who'd been *under my bed* stands up, still holding onto my calf.

I drop the bullet instantly and try to pull away, a shriek leaving me, and the rain picks that moment to pick up until it's splattering the roof and drowning out the noises of the crickets and frogs.

"You can go on and scream if you want, princess," the person says, resting one knee between my thighs on the bed. "I don't think anyone is going to hear you." I start to move, but he lunges forward, quick as a snake, until he can grip my throat and pin me in place with one leather-gloved hand. It gives me the unfortunate opportunity to see that the man is dressed all in black, with straps around the thighs of his black pants and a cowl over his shoulders and head that ends with a white mask, its slanted eyes large and almost comical staring me down.

"Oh my god," I gasp and look towards the closed door again. The dogs can't get in here. And my phone is over there as well. "Oh, my god-please–" I don't know what to do or say. I feel frozen and *trapped*. I feel stupid and terrified all at once; because of all the ways I've pictured myself going out, *masked campground serial killer* has never come into play.

"Not quite," the man purrs, his tone husky and smooth. In any other circumstance, I would *die* just to hear more of that voice. But tonight, I'd rather be anywhere but here. "Are you sure you don't want to scream?"

"Are you going to kill me?" I gasp, hands flying up to try to pry his fingers off my throat in a belated move for survival. He isn't pressing or choking. He's just *holding* me here when he could be doing much worse.

Though frankly, it's not that comforting.

The masked man tilts his head to the side, and I wonder if he's smiling behind the white visage. "No," he says after a moment, the word a soft growl. "I *was*," he goes on. And when I whimper, he brings his other hand up to cup my jaw. "*Shhh*. I *was*, I think. But I'm not going to kill you. I'm not going to hurt you, either."

"I don't believe you," I don't mean to say it, but the words slip out anyway. Since apparently, any sense of self-preservation I've ever had has gone out the window.

He chuckles softly in amusement and brushes his thumb over my lip. "I could've killed you a thousand times over," he points out. "And not just tonight. Think about that."

I don't want to, so I just stare at him instead.

"I'm not going to hurt you," he repeats. "But I really *want* what you've been offering me for the last couple of nights."

"Offering...you?" I ask, completely unaware of what he means, no matter how much I scour my brain for the answer. Am I stupid? *Have* I been sending out pen pal letters in my sleep, offering something stupid to inmates or serial killers? Or maybe *he's* just the crazy one. Yeah, that seems more likely.

"You're such a tease," he states, the hand on my face moving so he can skim his fingers down the front of my body. He catches the hem of my shirt and raises it, and suddenly I'm uncomfortably aware of his thigh pressed between mine. "I think you meant to be. What normal girl changes right in front of the window when she can't see what's outside?"

"It's the woods," I point out, unsure why I'm arguing with him. I catch his hand before he can lift my shirt over my breasts, and he lets me stop him. "There isn't...There shouldn't be anything in the woods."

"*I've* been in the woods," he points out. "Right outside your window. I thought you saw me that first night. But then you came in here and you got undressed right there." He lets out a sigh and twists his hand until he can twine his fingers with mine. It's surprisingly sweet and terrifying all at once.

"Tell me to stop," he invites. "Tell me you don't want me to give you what you want. I'm *not* going to hurt you, princess. I'll leave, and you can pretend this was just a nightmare."

"I..." With my heart pounding out a staccato rhythm in my chest that urges me on and fear making my fingers shake, I *absolutely* should tell him to leave. "Would you really leave? You're not *lying* to me just so I trust you, and you can stab me?"

"I'll really leave," he promises. "But you'll have to trust me on my word."

"I have no reason *to* trust you," I point out breathily, wishing I could sit up and think more clearly. "You broke into my cabin! I don't even know who you are."

"And you're not going to," the man continues. "My mask stays on. I want to play with you on my terms, princess. And my terms only. But I'm giving you a choice in that. Shall I stay, or shall I go?"

I need to tell him to leave. This is insane, like a dirty dream gone wrong, and the storm outside is making everything so much worse as thunder pounds in my brain like a drum.

He needs to leave.

If he really will.

"How do you know I'd even *consider* letting you stay?" I whisper when I should be screaming for him to leave. He's right that no one will hear me, though. And that thought is terrifying enough on its own.

The stranger's head tilts to the side. He lets go of my shirt and splays his hand against my stomach, moving it down until it rests just above the apex of my thighs. "Do you really want me to answer that for you?" he asks in an amused, almost-snicker.

Well, no. Not really. My thighs are still shaking, but curiosity and some kind of sick desire is warring with the fear in my chest.

I need to make him leave.

"It's so *hard*, isn't it," he goads, his hand above my thighs pressing against my skin. "It's so difficult when you know you should make me leave. I'm a monster, you know." I shudder, and his hand tightens slightly around my throat. "That's right, princess. I'm a really bad guy. And you can't tell me to stay, because what would that make you? A monster's plaything?"

It would be great if he could stop talking. It's hard to make the decision I know I need to make with his voice in my ears.

"How about this, sweet girl?" His hand drifts between my thighs until I feel the leather of his glove against my slit. "I won't make you say out loud that you're *interested* in what this monster has to offer you. Not this time. I'll let you tell me when you want me to stop. That's all you have to say. Just one word, and I'll be right back out that window before you can take another breath."

"Do you promise?" I hate the softness of my voice. I hate the way I feel like I'm asking for his approval.

"I don't make promises," he tells me. "But just this once, just for you, I'll make an exception, my little princess."

I look into the black eyes of his mask, lips pressed together, and whatever he sees in my face must give them the permission he seeks. His fingers sink into me, the leather sliding smoothly into my pussy as he leans over me and puts the smallest hint of pressure on my throat.

"That's a good girl," he praises. "I wasn't going to break in tonight." He pulls his fingers free as he speaks, and all I can think to do is stare at him. "But you had to play dirty, didn't you? Like you knew I'd be unable to resist."

I gasp, hips arching, as the bullet I'd dropped finds my clit. It's still on its middle setting, and I arch my hips as he teases me with it, the hand on my throat leaving so that he can push my hips back to the bed.

"I didn't know–"

"I think you knew," he goes on, humming the words. "You *invited* me to come on in, you know? When you turned that light on and spread your thighs so that I could see. Then when you showed me these..." He lifts my shirt, and this time I let him until my breasts spill free. "Like you were *begging* me to come play with you. You were even so kind as to get yourself so wet for me. But I would've done that for you, princess." He kneads my breast in his hand harder than I had, the leather of his gloves warm and smooth against my skin. "You didn't need to do any of this work for me. You could've just opened the window and got on the bed, and I would've done it all for you. Take your shirt off for me."

I lift up just enough so I can follow his instructions, and when I look up at him in the dim light, I can't help but feel like he's taking in the length of my body and all of my pale skin.

"Good girl," he praises, making my stomach twist. My thighs clench, and I can't help the way my hips jump just a little bit. "You like that, don't you? I knew you would. I knew how much you'd love it when I praised you. Will you earn more from me? I won't give it to you so easily now that I know you like it."

"I'm absolutely sure I don't know what you mean," I breathe, my voice barely above a whisper.

"Oh, is that how we're going to play this? Are you going to make *me* work for every little sound, every admittance from you? If you think I don't have the time or the *desire* to absolutely take you apart, I can assure you that you're *gravely* mistaken, princess."

It's the sweetest kind of threat I've ever heard.

"Or maybe you think that if you act like a little brat, that I'll get so frustrated I'll have to fuck you. Is that it? You want this stranger to just come in here and fuck this slutty pussy of yours?" I start to answer, but he reaches up to press his thumb against my lips. "*Shh*. I wasn't really asking. And I'm *not* going to fuck you. Not tonight. I don't think you want it bad enough."

When I make a soft sound of question, he chuckles. "You'll still enjoy everything I do to you, I promise. Though you don't get my cock tonight, princess. But that's okay. You've made sure I have *plenty* to work with." Something smooth and cool slides against my entrance when the bullet leaves my clit, and it takes me a few seconds to realize he's grabbed one of my other, larger toys from the drawer beside me.

I don't have time to say anything. Not that I'm sure what I would say. He slides the large toy into me until it's as deep as it can go, prompting me to gasp and arch into his grip.

"Do you always get this wet so easily?" the stranger whispers. "Or is it just because you love it when I play with you so much?" His thumb encircles my clit again, and he teases me while letting the large toy just *rest* inside of me without even turning it on. "That's not rhetorical, princess," he adds, his other hand pinching my nipple suddenly. "Which are you? A horny little slut, or do you just love having a masked stranger come in and play with your pussy that much?"

It doesn't feel like there's a right answer. I writhe, my hands going to his wrist as he switches to tease my other nipple. "I'm not a slut," I say finally, but that's not a real answer.

He shoves me down when I start to sit up. "Hands over your head. You can grip the headboard, princess." He waits until I do what he says. My fingers tangle in the pillowcase over my head as I watch him as well as I can. "If you're not a little slut, then that means you're the second one, right?" He uses both of his thighs to press mine apart, and when his hand presses against my stomach, I'm effectively trapped. I can't do *anything* other than gasp and jerk my hips when he turns on the toy inside me as high as it'll go.

"That means you *love* this, princess. It means that I could've come in here whenever I wanted and done *everything* I've wanted to do these last few nights. You were never going to stop me, were you?" If he expects an answer, he doesn't give me time to do so. He pumps the toy in and out of me, pushing it as deep as it'll go before dragging it back out. "That's fine," he adds, and a few moments later, the bullet is teasing my clit again. He holds both toys in one hand as he fucks me, still managing to hit both my clit and the inside of my pussy *perfectly* like he's practiced it. "That's more than fine, actually. Because I don't want you to be like this for just anyone." His movement picks up, and his hand on my stomach presses me down harder so that I really can't go anywhere. "You'd better be like this just for *me*. You got that, princess?"

I don't have much of anything, honestly, except for a brain and body full of pleasure as he fucks me better than I ever have with my toys. All I can focus on is not *screaming* right now and keeping my hands fisted in the blankets above me.

"*You got that?*" he snarls, face closer to mine than I expected it to be.

"Yes!" I gasp, opening my eyes that I hadn't known I'd closed.

"Then come for me. Right now. You can do it. Come for me, all over your toys and my hand. *Don't make me tell you again.*"

Before the last words leave his lips, I'm coming, my body arching off the bed as I finally *do* scream, though it's not with fear but mind-blowing pleasure. My toes curl, and I close my eyes again as he teases me through my orgasm, reducing me to a Sloane-shaped puddle on the mattress.

God, I need a minute, or an hour, just for my brain to process what's going on. I'm pretty sure I've never come so hard in my life, and I'm grateful when he turns off both toys, though he keeps the larger one inside me and tosses the bullet onto the bed.

"Holy fuck," I mutter, throwing my head back and taking a deep, shuddering breath. With my eyes closed, I find myself spacing out, and I could probably fall asleep *right now* if there wasn't a masked psycho running his gloved hand up my body between my breasts.

"Don't get too comfortable, princess," he purrs, hand going to my throat again. "We're not done yet."

My eyes fly open, and I look into the black eyes of his mask, but when I try to sit up, he pushes me back down with the hand on my throat and straddles my waist. "*What?*" I demand like he's going to pull a knife and murder me anyway.

The stranger chuckles as he keeps me on the bed with his weight and his hand on my throat. "Don't look at me like that. You've spent the last three nights teasing me. I deserve at least another hour with your pretty body. Especially your sweet pussy. Don't you think that's fair?" When I start to answer, his other hand covers my mouth once more. "*That* was a rhetorical question," he says. "The only things you're allowed to say are yes, harder, *please,* and more."

7

A part of me wants to believe that everything that happened during the night was a fever dream. That no one broke in through the now-replaced screen. That a masked man *didn't* give me the best orgasms of my life before slipping back out the way he'd come.

He'd never fucked me, though. I'm *pretty sure* I begged for it at some point, but the stranger had just chuckled and told me I didn't want it bad enough. *Which was super fucking rude, honestly.*

A dog whines and I let out a sigh as one of them paws at the closed door of the bedroom. Dang it. They've both been out in the main room of the cabin all night instead of in here with me like they usually are.

Slowly I stand, stretching, and when I glance at the window once more, I see that not only has the screen been replaced, the curtain has been drawn. I sure as hell didn't do that. Not to mention, I'm not even sure when my new friend *left*. Had I passed out by then?

It seems pretty likely.

Quickly, I pull on my clothes for the day, dressing in black leggings, a long pink tee, and my light zip-up hoodie with the thumb holes. With the storm yesterday, and the one last night, there's a good chance I'll be cleaning up debris. I'd rather not do that in shorts.

After I toe on my shoes, I go to the window and reach my hand up to grip the curtain, hesitating as I do.

But I'm really not going to let him dictate what I do with my window. I *yank* the curtain open and stare out into the woods, scanning the trees for any sign of his white mask or *any* kind of movement at all.

My eyes find nothing, however. Whether he's there and I just can't see him, or he has a life during the day, I don't see anyone in my woods waiting to see what I do with my curtain.

"What the actual fuck..." I mumble, not genuinely asking the question, but also, *what the fuck?* Part of me absolutely *is* willing to believe this was a fever dream because who does that? Better yet, who *has this happen to them?*

Outside of a movie, anyway. And most horror movies I've seen definitely don't go the same way my night did.

Opening the door, I'm not surprised when both dogs barrel inside, Vulcan's nose going to the ground while Argus launches himself up to my chest and pushes me back a step. He whines and licks my face, his tail wagging as he sniffs me for any damage or change.

"I'm okay," I promise him, kissing his nose loudly. "I'm okay, I promise." I almost wasn't okay, maybe? But what matters is that I'm fine now.

"Do you guys want a snick-snack?" I ask, baby-talking my adult, fully grown, highly trained canines. Both of them look up at the word, and Argus drops down to stand in front of me, wiggling his butt at the implication of food.

"Let's go get a snick-snack." They follow me out into the

kitchen, and I grab the bag of large chews off the counter. It's a new bag, thankfully, since the two of them can go through a bag in a week, and I give both dogs a large treat before going to the door and opening it into the overcast morning.

Rain drips audibly through the trees as I step outside, the dogs following and then wandering off to do their morning routine of sniff, pee, sniff.

I can't help but walk around to the back of the cabin, gazing at the screen and into my room, where I can clearly see my bed. I take a few steps back, only stopping when I'm at the edge of the trees and then a few more until I'm just in the woods.

How close had the masked stranger been? How long had he stayed, looking in my window for the past few nights? It's unfathomable to me that someone could just *be* here like this, especially in the middle of nowhere, but I suppose that in itself makes the feat easier for him.

My phone goes off in my hoodie pocket, making me lurch in surprise and nearly trip over a root as I stumble back down to the flatter ground around the cabin. "Hello?" I ask the phone to my ear. I hadn't bothered to check who it was, so it really could be just about anyone, and here I am, just answering the phone without any kind of caution.

"Oh good, you're up." Sam lets out a long sigh. "*As we thought, two-fourteen got hit again. But we're going to take care of that. Can you go along the ridge and check out all the campers there? Most of 'em aren't here this week, and I worry. Then check the lodge back there too. The beach probably looks like shit, so just take a picture for me...*" she trails off, sounding worn out even though it's barely seven-thirty in the morning.

"Do you still want me to go up to Highland and the streets up there?" I ask, wondering if that plan has changed.

"*Nah. But go up the hill behind the House. I know it's mostly temporaries for the week, but I'd like to make sure there's nothing blocking the road or anything. Okay?"*

"No problem," I agree, whistling, so the dogs stop wandering and start following me down the incline towards the main area of the campground. "I'm just leaving the cabin, so I'll be just a few minutes before I get there."

Sam chuckles. *"When are you going to pick up the keys to one of the golf carts and just start driving those?"*

I shudder. "I don't think I'm the golf cart type," I tell her with a snicker in my voice. "Besides, can you see Vulcan *actually* riding in one of them?" Argus, of course, would have no issue laying wherever I put him, even if that were on a golf cart, but I'd be lucky if Vulcan didn't climb up to the roof and bay his displeasure to the hills.

She snorts. "*All right. See you when I see you.*" She hangs up, and I shove the phone into my pocket, my strides lengthening so that I can feel the full privilege of being almost five-foot-nine.

Minutes pass, and I duck into the House for only a moment, just long enough to make sure Sam's niece is working at the counter. She glances up from her phone and shoots me a tired smile, waving as she does.

"Hey," I call, pouring myself a blue-raspberry slushie. "You okay?"

"I'm just tired," she croaks, sounding like she's been awake for the last ten years instead of, most likely, an hour. "How do you get up this early every day?"

"Long practice and having dogs who *want* to be up this early," I tell her, flashing her a quick smile on my way back out. "See you later."

"Later." She goes back to her phone before I'm even out the door. Not that Sam or Pat really care. They only have her work when it's dead, or they're not expecting people to check in or out. Given that it's Wednesday, I can absolutely see their reasoning for having her here today.

I round the side of the House on the opposite side from where I came from, the dogs ranging around the area, when I see Vulcan suddenly turn, his ears perk and his tail wagging. He's not looking at me, however, and I follow his gaze to see *Virgil* walking up from the dock, dressed in jeans and a short-sleeved tee that shows off more of the black tattoos that climb his arm from his fingers.

When Vulcan meets him at the top of the sidewalk, he grins, one hand going out to scratch my dog's ears as his eyes unerringly find my face.

I don't say anything. Instead, I suck on the straw of the slushie, my cheeks half hollowed as I gaze at him and wait for him to speak.

But he takes a moment, appraising my expression, and looks back down at Vulcan before he *does* say something. "You're a *good boy*," he tells my dog like they're old friends. "You make me miss my dog."

"You have a dog?" I ask, surprised he hasn't brought it with him.

"Nah, not anymore." His eyes flick back to mine. "My friend has a couple of cats, but I don't have any pets right now. You make me want to change that."

Argus sits down beside me, and I reach down to give him the same flavor of attention that Vulcan is getting.

"Good morning, by the way," he adds when I don't say anything else.

"Good morning." I look down at the dock and pinpoint his shiny red and white boat instantly. "Were you out fishing?"

"Just out on the lake," he shrugs. "I like it better when it's not so crowded in the morning. The storms are clearing up for the day, so I'm sure in a few hours, it'll be packed out there."

He's not wrong, from my experience.

"Did you see any storm damage?" I keep my tone conversational, and I try to hide the way my eyes go back to the tattoos around his arm that are obscured just enough by him standing there that I can't tell what they are. Especially the one on his hand that looks like it wraps around his wrist and ends somewhere near the base of his ring finger.

"It's a snake," he replies, most certainly not answering my question.

My eyes flick up to his, bemusement making me tilt my head. "What?"

"My tattoo that you're staring at." He approaches me, hand out in front of him to show me the snake tattoo that wraps around his wrist. "See?"

Oh.

"Did it hurt?" I want to reach out and touch it, to trace the pattern of scales that end on his forearm.

"Not really. The ones on my chest did when the needle went across my collarbone. But other than that, they weren't bad either."

Unbidden, my eyes flick up to the dark gray of his tee, and I almost wish I could see through the fabric to see the tattoo underneath.

I also want to see what he'd do if I asked him to show me, but based on the unpredictability of our conversations, he really might.

But would that be such a bad thing?

"You look tired," Virgil continues, dropping his hand to his side. "Long night? Did the storm keep you up?"

"Boring night," I reply, not looking up at his face as I take another long drink of my slushie. "I couldn't fall asleep, but nothing really happened."

"Yeah?" he chuckles. "I like storms, but the one last night

was something else. I was up in the loft all night wondering if my cabin was going to get blown away."

I snort and look up at his face finally, surprised that we're not more than four inches apart in height. He's about six-foot, but just barely, and I'm close enough to eye level that I can easily see the gold flecks in his hazel eyes.

"I like them too," I admit. "And you actually slept in the *loft*? Those beds are tiny."

"They're not so bad. Not like there's anyone other than me."

"You're too tall for them."

"I scrunched."

The stupid response makes me snort out a laugh, and I cover my mouth to try to lessen the collateral damage of nearly spitting out my slushie. Forcibly I swallow, lessening the chance of coughing all over his shirt, but keep my mouth covered for a few more seconds until I'm sure I can control myself.

Virgil grins at me, waiting for me to recover, and thankfully doesn't say anything about it. "Where are you going?" he asks, letting Vulcan push between us so that the man is forced to pay attention to him.

It distracts me from the question, and I look down at my dog in confusion. "I don't get it," I tell him. "Vulcan is weird about strangers. Obviously, he likes you, but this is next level. Did you sneak him some peanut butter while I wasn't looking or something?"

"Why peanut butter?" He scratches the dog's chin, making faces at him like Vulcan's a baby. Though I can't criticize when I'm just as guilty of babying the dogs.

"He loves peanut butter. I can't figure out why else he'd be so in love with you." I shrug my shoulders and take a few steps back, glancing towards the ridge that overlooks the lake and is lined with campers. "Anyway, I gotta go. I have to check for storm damage to the campers along the road."

"Can I come?" He asks it so smoothly and without any kind of hesitation that I'm caught off guard by the request.

"Sure?" I mean to tell him no. He does not need to go walking around the campground looking for damage with me, but instead, what comes out is *sure*.

What the fuck, brain-to-mouth filter?

"Oh, wow. I thought you'd say no."

"Well, if you don't want to go—"

His smile is wicked, and he cuts me off with a chuckle. "I wouldn't have asked if I didn't, Sloane."

The way he says my name is always such a nice thing to hear. I blink up at him and shrug one shoulder, not wanting to look *too* enthused. "Hope you like picking up *trees*," I tell him and set off down the ridge.

"I don't," he says cheerfully. "But I kind of like you, so picking up the trees is worth suffering through."

I nearly trip over my own feet at that and turn to glance at him over my shoulder as he catches up to walk beside me. "You're so weird," I say, unable to think of anything else that doesn't involve me staring at him and slurping my slushie like an awkward teenager.

"Oh, I *know*," he agrees enthusiastically. "But as it turns out, I'm starting to think you *like it* a little bit, don't you?"

8

By the time Virgil is back wherever the hell he goes when he's not spoiling Vulcan, and I'm done cleaning up the mess from the storm, it's late afternoon and I'm ready for food. And sleep, but mostly food.

When I do eat, it's at my cabin, with the campfire going, and the heat from it washes over my bare legs as I sit in a camp chair and stare up at the sky. Having cleaned up and changed a few hours ago, I'm glad I'm in my shorts and t-shirt while sitting this close to the fire. The storms have rolled past for now, and it'll be days before it storms again, according to the weatherman. For now, I can see the stars as the crickets and frogs sing in the woods, filling my ears along with the sounds of the crackling campfire.

I still haven't called my mom. It's easy during the day to forget about my stepfather calling me. It's easy to be only distantly upset, unsure and to hold onto the idea that I need to call Mom *eventually*. It's not like I can call her while I'm dragging limbs out of the road, after all. Or while I'm ankle-deep in the mud trying to move debris out of the path to the playground.

But right now, when it's just me and the campfire and my dogs, it's impossible to feel anything but guilty for not getting that one thing done. She deserves to know. Even though it raises panic in my chest to think about dealing with it or what will come of things, I *need* to call her and get it done.

At my side Argus flops over with a sigh, staring up at me for a moment as if he can sense the invisible black clouds that hang over me as I lose myself deeper and deeper in thought.

It didn't help that I'd come back to the cabin after work and promptly fell asleep. After last night and the work I'd done with Virgil at my side today, all I'd wanted to do was *nap*. And that nap turned into a five-hour sleep session that will probably keep me up all night. Even now, it's nearly midnight, and I couldn't be more wired than I am, though my slack pose is anything but.

Of course, it doesn't help that I'm hyper-aware of the woods around me. Is my masked stranger out there biding his time as he watches me sit by the fire? Maybe he'll kill me tonight, instead.

The thought makes me shudder with the barely repressed fear and anticipation that courses through my body, warring with the bad feelings my stepfather calling has left behind like a bitter aftertaste.

Or maybe the stranger is bored of me after last night, and he's gone to find some other girl to stalk. I can't imagine I'm *that* interesting to warrant a second visit. Though I'm still unsure what I did to merit the first.

"You guys were a big help last night," I murmur to the dogs, sitting up finally to stare into the fire that's died down considerably over the last hour. "Couldn't even tell me he was coming?"

In response, Vulcan gets up and heads behind the cabin, padding on steady paws into the woods around us.

Since I'm out here, I'm not worried. I'll hear him if he tries to take off after anything, and even though he's been going into the woods more, he still isn't trying to run *away*. As per usual, Argus couldn't care less. He lets out another groan, and I reach down to lightly toy with his ears, making them twitch a few times before he lifts a paw to rub them and chase my hand away.

"Sorry," I chuckle, getting to my feet and poking the fire to settle it. It's almost out, and it takes me only a few minutes of work and a gallon of water to have the fire completely gone and cool enough that I don't mind getting up and leaving it.

"Vulc?" I call, still able to hear the dog behind the cabin, just at the edge of the woods. He comes back to me, tail wagging, and lets me give him a quick chin rub before he goes to the door and waits. It's an easily readable sign from him that he's ready to go in, and I guess I am too. I might as well be, anyway. I can at least binge some bad TV before I go to sleep, though I'm sure I'll end up falling asleep on the couch tonight instead of the bed.

Should I just get naked and go sprawl on the bed? Just in case?

Absolutely not, I reprimand my brain. *You are not asking for it like that.*

Though I'm not sure why not, since last night had been *literally* the best sex of my life even though my masked stranger had never touched me skin-to-skin. *Or* actually fucked me.

Checking the fire once more, I walk to the door and push it open, allowing the dogs to spill inside and go immediately to the couch as if telling me that it's *their* bed for the night instead of mine.

"I could push you off," I remind them, closing the door

behind me. I probably *will* push them off too, but at the moment, I smell too much like smoke to do anything other than change.

On instinct, when I walk into my room, I look at the window that faces the woods. The screen is still completely in place, making me sigh in relief.

Relief, and totally not disappointment.

I *will not* be disappointed over the absence of a *murderer* in my cabin who may or may not see through on his promise of not killing me if he shows up again.

Just to be safe, and because I'm absolutely asking for it at this point, I get on my knees and flip the comforter up from the floor, peering under it and using the light from the room to make sure there's no one under there waiting to drag me under or loom over me when I go to bed.

It, too, is free of strangers. Masked or otherwise.

With a groan, I push myself to my feet and chuck my phone onto the dresser by the door. Since I *am* alone, there's no point in doing anything other than going right back to my couch and letting myself drift into a half-vegetative state for the rest of the night. Just because I'm not tired doesn't mean I won't be able to pass the night only vaguely conscious.

It takes only a few quick movements before I'm out of my clothes, and when I go to grab my pj's off the end of the bed, I stop.

They were totally there this morning. They're *always* there, and I'm not stupid enough to think that they got up and moved themselves.

"I checked under the bed," I say, glaring at the end of it. "And the window is closed. If I look up and you're stuck to the ceiling or swinging on the fan, I'm going to be *so* upset and probably a little bit impressed."

A chuckle behind me makes my stomach lurch, but I can't exactly say that I'm *surprised*.

Was he in my closet?

"Some girls are just so cocky after a night getting fucked by their own toys," the masked stranger purrs. I hear the shifting of clothes, and I don't need to look to know that he's *right* there. "Should I show you that it's not safe to be so confident around me?"

My insides twist, and I do turn to look at him, glad I'm still wearing my underwear as I cross my arms over my chest as if I suddenly care about him seeing me naked.

I should care. This is so fucked up, the danger of unaliving or not. He's a stranger, and I don't even know what his face looks like. He's probably a murderer, judging by what he's said. I should *not* be okay with him being here.

He must see the trepidation in my face because the stranger holds up his hands to show me they're empty. "Same rules apply, princess," he tells me in that low, husky voice that shoots heat to my core. "You tell me to stop or leave, and I will. All right?"

"You promise?" I ask again, unable to move until he *promises.* As if this is some binding magic that'll mean he can't hurt me when in fact, he could break such a stupid promise at any time if he wanted to.

He steps out of the closet, black boots making only a slight, soft sound on the carpet, and reaches out to me with one gloved hand curled into a fist, pinky extended. "Would you like me to *pinky swear?*" he asks, only a small bit of amusement in his tone. "Will that make you feel better?"

I stare at his hand and snort softly, lifting my hand to curl my finger around his. I feel like a little kid when I do it, but I still do it all the same.

"Now go close your door," he encourages, tilting his

masked face towards it to make his point. "I don't need your dogs coming after me when I make you scream."

"Are you afraid of them?" I don't know why I ask, but I walk to the door and close it anyway. The two dogs gaze at me, Argus thumping his tail as the door closes like the *worst* kind of chaperone.

"Not in the least." There's amusement in his voice, and I keep the bed between us as I wait for him to keep going. "But things happen, and I don't feel like getting bit tonight. Are you going to get on the bed, or am I going to *make* you?"

The threat sends a shiver up my spine that I'm not convinced is fear. Because my brain is working in overdrive, putting pieces together as I stare at him. "Vulcan would've torn you apart if he scented you in here," I murmur, folding my arms over my chest again. "He doesn't like people that much. And it's not like he *knows* you."

The masked stranger just watches me.

"Why isn't my dog trying to kill you? Why didn't he try to kill you last night, either?" I ask finally, my words slow as I try to answer my own question.

A soft snicker is his only reply. "What makes you think I have any intention of answering your questions? Besides, what does it matter? I'm in here, aren't I?" He tilts his head to look at my black comforter that's only barely covering part of the bed, then back at me. "And the longer you stand there, the more I think you *want* me to play rough with you."

My heart does a flip at the thought, and I slant my eyes to the side. I probably don't want that.

Probably.

"Oh, *princess*," he sneers, his voice utterly mocking. "That's so fucked up. You don't even know who I *am*." As I watch, he moves slowly around the bed until he stands on the same side of it as I do. One hand snakes out, and he grips my throat lightly, the cool leather of his glove sliding against my skin. "Have you ever used a safeword while you play?"

"No," I whisper, my eyes finding the black gaze of his mask. "I...I know the premise, though. And the concept doesn't seem difficult to grasp."

"In this case, I'm wondering if you'd want to use one with me to tell me to stop. Would you like that? We can *pretend* that you don't like it. We'll *pretend* that you don't want to be on this bed while I wreck you tonight like I did last night. You can tell me to stop all you want, but I won't. *If* you want to have a safeword instead."

I suck in a breath, unsure of his words. It sounds like something I want to try, no doubt. Because the idea of him pinning me down and doing *anything* to me is quite appealing, and so is the idea of playing hard to get, for lack of a better term.

"What if I forget it? Or I say stop instead, and I *mean* stop?" I ask, second-guessing myself *and* my tenuous decision.

"We'll use *red*. That's pretty hard to forget, and I doubt you'll be saying it in any other context. Other than that..." He shrugs and lifts his other hand to drag me forward, hand on my thigh. "I suppose you'd have to trust that I can see if you'll really need to stop. I'm not going to do anything that'll hurt you. Though if there's something I need to know before we play, I guess this *would* be the time to tell me."

"Trust you?" I repeat, unsure of how I feel about those words from him.

He dips his face in a nod.

"You won't even show me your face."

"Oh, I know. It's just so unfair, isn't it?"

"What if I took your mask off? Would you kill me?"

"You won't." There's no question in his words. No possibility of anything other than me simply not doing it.

"I...won't?"

The hand on my hip comes up to cup my jaw, and he *yanks* me forward so that we're pressed together. "You won't," he assures me. "Even this close, you *won't*. Do you know why?"

I'm sure I don't, though my racing heart makes it hard to think of anything when he's this close to me. I shake my head slightly, only barely managing to make it look like something other than a spasm.

"Because I told you not to. And at your core, you're such a good fucking girl, aren't you, princess?"

"I have a name." I can't help but say it. Does he not know? Would he use it if he did?

"I know. But I don't need your name when I'd rather call you *princess*. Though maybe tonight you'll be my little slut instead." He moves to grip my jaw instead of my throat, and his other hand settles on my hip once more. "I'm tired of talking. Shall we continue with 'stop,' or would you like to use 'red' instead when you need me to stop?"

I shouldn't complicate things. I don't need to complicate things when this is already dangerous enough. Adding an aspect to our game just feels like a test. Like I might be throwing myself into the deep end when I really shouldn't.

"I want to use red," I say, my mouth betraying my common sense.

I get the feeling he's grinning in approval, though I can't see if he is. "That's my good girl," he says and then *throws* me back onto the bed, fingers hooking in my panties and jerking them off my legs before I can do more than gasp.

I sit up, surprised, only for him to catch me by the hair and jerk me off the bed and down to my knees harshly.

"Stay down there where you belong, princess. Being on your knees is a good look for you." He lets go of my hair and unzips his pants, the leather never catching on the zipper as he pulls his black jeans down just enough to free his already hard cock. "You're going to let me fuck your mouth, aren't you?" It doesn't feel like he's genuinely asking. Especially when he grips my hair and urges me forward. "You're going to let me use that pretty little mouth however I want, and then I'll fuck that pussy when I'm done. That's what you *want*, isn't it?" His grip tightens in my hair, and I realize that he wants an answer.

"Yes," I murmur, looking up at him through my lashes.

"That wasn't very convincing. If you want something, you ask me *nicely* with a please attached. Try again."

"Yes, *please*."

"Please *what?*"

My face burns, and I swallow, trying to formulate the words that feel humiliating to say out loud. "I want you to fuck my mouth—"

"And *what else?*"

"And my pussy. *Please*."

"There you go." The stranger's fingers loosen in my hair, and he gives me time to wrap my fingers around the base of his length, my tongue licking over his crown. He's *bigger* than I expect him to be, and it's hard not to imagine how he'll feel when he's fucking me.

"Don't get lost in your little dream world now, princess. I want to feel those lips around my cock before I fill your pussy. Got that?"

I don't answer. Not verbally, anyway. My eyes flick up to his, and I take him in my mouth, letting him urge me further down until the weight of him rests on my tongue.

It's a damn good thing I don't have a gag reflex. Especially since he's big enough that I can feel him in my throat, and it's enough to make my eyes slightly water.

It's also more than enough to make my own body ache. Part of me considers reaching down to use my fingers, but that *definitely* seems like something he won't like.

"Good girl," he praises, letting me draw away slightly. "I knew your mouth would feel good. You look like you were made to take my cock in all of your holes." I shudder at that, and he chuckles. "Do you like the sound of that? Should I keep going after I fill your pussy? Should I fuck your ass as well? I bet no one else ever has." He grips my hair with both hands and keeps me in place so that he can draw out and then slide back in.

"Stay right like that. Right there." He thrusts as deep as he can and groans, fucking my throat while I try hard to suck in breaths through my nose.

It's not enough, though. I need more air than he's giving me, and my hand flies up to curl around his jean-clad thigh.

I'm going to need to *breathe* soon.

"I know, *I know*," he assures me, not doing anything to give me relief. "But I'm not done. You hear me? You're going to stay right there *because I'm not fucking done with that mouth*."

I whine around him, tears gathering in my eyes and cascading down my cheeks as black spots start to obscure my vision while he fucks my mouth. Finally, when I'm half sure I'm going to pass out, he lets go and steps back, my jaw falling slack as my mouth is suddenly empty, and I'm able to *finally* breathe in deep gasps of air.

I don't expect him to pull me onto the bed, one hand on my jaw while the other holds my thigh. "Good girl," he purrs, masked face close to mine like he wants to kiss me. "You're so good for me, but I knew you would be. Ever since I first saw you, I *knew* you would be so good for me. Get on my lap. I want to fucking look at you." He tugs me over his thighs, forcing me to straddle him, and my breasts brush the front of his jacket as I do, my eyes at the level of the black eyes of his mask.

His fingers skim up my sides, making me writhe, and I

whine softly in protest. "Tickling isn't sexy," I tell him, my voice just a little bit hoarse.

"You make everything sexy," he disagrees and does it again. As he does so, he shifts so that one of his thighs is pressed against me. "Why don't you use my thigh to get yourself a little more worked up for me, hmm? Don't use your hands. Put them around my shoulders." I do so, sliding them around his shoulders so I'm forced to be almost nose-to-nose with the white mask. "Right there. That's so good. Now just rock your hips. C'mon. You know what to do, don't you?"

It's awkward, in a way. But I can't deny how hot it is to ride his denim-clad leg with nothing between me and the rough fabric. Every time my clit slides over it just right, I shudder, and I'm sure that his jeans are going to be wet after this.

One of his hands lands on my thigh, urging me to keep going, while the other reaches to cup my jaw.

"I just can't help myself with you," he tells me quietly. I turn my face into his hand, mouth open as he presses his thumb to my lips, and open my eyes to see the band of tan skin between his jacket and his glove.

And the black ink there that curls around his wrist.

I blink, and as if he knows what I'm looking at, he pulls away with a rueful sigh.

"I want to watch you get off like this, I bet you could, couldn't you? But I'm so fucking ready to bury myself in your pussy. Do you understand?" His hand moves to grip my hair, and he pulls me upright to look at his mask again. "Once I'm inside you, then you don't get a say," he purrs. "You'll be all mine, then. Does that scare you?"

"Yes," I say without hesitation.

"Oh, it should. It should *terrify* you, princess. You should never have let me stay. I have a lifetime to ruin you, and you've given me permission." Before I can reply, he uses his grip on my hair to push me onto the bed, getting out from under me and shoving me hard onto my stomach, my face buried in my pillows.

I gasp and try to sit up, my head spinning, only for him to pin me there with a snarl.

"No, you stay *right there*. Facedown, but get your hips up right now." He grabs my thighs and forces me to my knees, though my face is still on the bed where he put me. "This is how you should've been waiting for me. Understand?" His leather-clad hand comes down hard on my upper thigh with a resounding *smack*.

I yelp and this time, I *do* sit up, only for him to grab me by my hair and *snarl* in my ear.

"I said *stay*," he reminds me, his voice so close to a growl that I can't help but shudder. "This isn't you staying, is it? And it's most certainly not how I put you."

"I wasn't expecting–"

"*I didn't ask,*" he cuts me off with finality and presses me down onto the bed once more, albeit more gently than I'd expected. "Like I *said*." He grabs my thighs and pulls them wider apart so that I can't hold myself up with any kind of good balance. "This is how you should've been waiting for me tonight. Not with your clothes on. And you shouldn't be making me wait." His gloves hands run up my thighs, then back down. "How tight will you be if I take you right now without opening you up?"

"Please don't," I whisper, though my heart races with something that's absolutely not fear.

"Please *don't?*" He leans over me, and I can feel his cock slide against my folds, eliciting a whimper from me. His mask skims along my shoulder blade, and in a kinder voice, he murmurs, you remember your safe word, right, Sloane?"

The use of my name almost shocks me out of the moment,

and I have to take a second to pull myself together. More shockingly, he lets me. One hand rubs comfortingly over my hip, but he doesn't rush me or move forward with anything while I get my bearings.

"Yes," I whisper.

"What is it?" There's something different in his voice. Something other than his mocking praise or growled threats.

"Red."

"Do you need to use it?"

I swallow back the confusion and rush of surprise, balling my hands in my sheets. It's...thoughtful. It's almost sweet, though I'll never say that out loud. "No," I say after taking stock of my mental state. "I'm not using it."

The mask brushes my skin again, and this time his murmured, "good girl," is somehow different enough that I can *feel* the affection in his words. That, or I'm just hallucinating, which is certainly more likely.

"Oh, *princess*," he continues, back to the voice I expect from him as he pulls back. "You don't really want me to stop. You want me to fuck your pussy just like this, don't you? Look how *wet* you are." He spreads my folds with two fingers so he can look at me, and I whimper. "You're fucking *begging* me to just wreck you."

"I'm not. I'm–"

"You are. You want my cock right now? You want me to fuck you without doing anything to get you ready for me?"

"No. I don't. I–" The words fall from my lips, and I don't mean them because I know my limits enough to know how I feel about *this*, but it's somehow frightening in the best way all the same. I swallow a whine when his cock rubs against my slit, and I can feel him lining himself up with me before he grips my hip once more.

"Yeah, you really fucking do." With those words, he thrusts

into me, sliding slowly as he parts my folds with his cock, and I cry out, writhing under him with my face still in the pillow and my hands fisted in the sheets above it.

"You're so tight," he tells me, only coming to a halt when his body is pressed against mine, and I can *feel* him incredibly deep. "God, I'm not going to be able to last long when you're so tight and *hot*." He pulls back and thrusts in again, a little faster this time, and the stretch of him is almost too much.

Almost, but just perfectly on the edge of too much that it feels *amazing*.

"Is that too much, princess?" He moves again, but this time he doesn't stop when he's deep inside me only continues to fuck me as his hips pick up their rhythm.

"Yes."

"*No*, I don't think it is. Your pussy is just *begging* me to be here. It's not too much at all." With a hand on my lower back, he holds me in place, using me as his thrusts become harder and the burn of him fades into hot pleasure.

He isn't the only one that isn't going to last long. He's impossibly hot, and it feels *so fucking good* to have him inside me that I wonder if this really might be a strangely lucid fever dream.

When the buzzing starts, I barely notice. It's when my bullet finds my clit that I come back to the moment with a shriek and try to bolt upright, only for him to keep me in place.

"Oh *fuck,* that feels good. That's right. You're so *tight* around me when I play with your clit. Are you going to come?" I am if he keeps doing that. "I asked you a *question*."

"I'm gonna come," I tell him, opening my mouth and finding that now I can't stop my rambling. "Fuck, I'm gonna come so fast. That's too much–"

"Not if I say it's not." He's fucking into me harder now, and the force of his thrusts makes the vibrator slide over my clit deliciously as he hits so deep inside me that I feel like I'm seeing stars. "Come for me." He slaps my thigh, the hot pain going right to my clit. "Come on. You shouldn't need me to tell you more than once. I want to feel you come on my cock, princess. I don't think that's too much to ask."

He's not really asking, though. And when he repeats the words with the vibrator on my clit, I can't help but tumble over the edge into my orgasm. I gasp, spine arching, and he fucks me through it, still playing with my clit even when it becomes too much as my body clenches around him.

"Stop," I beg, writhing on the bed and trying to get my knees under me to jerk away from the intense sensations. My muscles still flutter as he drags out my orgasm, but God, it's *too much*. "Please stop, just for a second—"

"No. Absolutely not." His hand tightens on my hip as he fucks me. "You're going to take everything I give you. You're going to take everything I *tell you* to take, do you hear me? But beg me to stop. Maybe it'll make a difference, princess. Fucking *beg me*."

I do. Pleas and whines fall from my lips as he fucks me through another orgasm, this one stronger than the first, and when I have a third, smaller one, I find that I'm *crying* while my thighs shake and struggle to hold me up. It's only his grip that keeps me in place, and finally, during my third orgasm, he drops the vibrator and grabs both my hips to slam into me, his pace becoming erratic as he growls his version of praise.

"I can't believe how perfect you are for me," the stranger tells me, on the cusp of his own orgasm and his voice tight. "I should've been fucking this pussy for days now. *God*, you never should've let me stay, you know that?" He thrusts once more, burying himself deep in my body as he comes. "I'm going to make you regret it," he laughs, the sound grating and somewhat terrifying as it feels like a promise. "God, you're going to regret it so much when I wreck you over and over until you're ruined for anyone other than me."

I don't know what to say. With my eyes closed against my pillow and tears drying on my face from how much he's pushed my body, all I can do is replay his words over in my head and wonder if he's serious.

And if he is, how *fucked* that makes me.

9

"Sorry," I tell the dogs, giving them a handful of treats in apology for them spending another night on the couch. It doesn't seem like they mind, exactly. Not when I know they like the couch almost as much as snuggling up with me. "I'm sorry," I say again, and I push the door open to let them out as they finish chowing down on their food. I probably owe them a pup cup as well, and since I'm going into town, it'll be the best opportunity I have to grab one for each dog.

It's a good thing that the only things I *have* to do today consist of going into town and picking up a few things for the House. We're running low, and thanks to some issues with transportation in Arkala, sometimes I get to go pick up what we sell, like t-shirts, instead of us having them delivered. I don't mind. I like driving, and I like an excuse to go into Arkala to get something from the bakery that also serves way better coffee than any franchise store ever could.

"Come on boys," I say, fighting the urge to go check the woods behind the cabin again. Thoughts about my nighttime visitor swirl around in my brain, and while most of them are *good*, there are a few that make my insides clench.

Is he who I think he is? Do I really want the answer to that when it feels like maybe he's trying to keep himself unknown so that *I* can't get attached? And how in the world does he keep getting past Vulcan without the dog doing so much as growling or barking to let me know he's here?

Vulcan only lets people pass who he likes. Which doesn't say much about their character, but it *does* tell me that the man can magically phase in and out of my cabin, is a hallucination, or somehow has earned Vulc's affection.

None of them are very likely when I certainly don't let my dog waltz up to just everyone. The only people he *does* like are campers, only the frequent visitors at that, and I have a hard time imagining that chubby, grill-obsessed Benjamin is behind that mask or old, hobbling Carter.

I close the back door of my silver Hyundai Elantra and slide into the front seat, plugging my phone into the jack before turning the key in the ignition. The nice part of not having to pay anything towards rent or a mortgage means that I've been able to afford a nicer car than I had before, and if I breathe *really* deeply and pretend a little, I like to think that I can still smell that new car scent, instead of just dog.

Smoothly I pull out of my parking area and onto the road, creeping along the rough asphalt until I get to the House where Sam and Pat are working today. Surreptitiously I check for Virgil's truck, though I don't see it here, and when I look for his boat on the dock, I see that it's sitting in its spot, right where it belongs.

Do I walk a loop around the cabins to see if he's still there? I don't know why he would've left early, and I *really* don't need him to think I'm stalking him.

As a compromise, I crane my head back, looking for any

sign of the large, shiny black truck. And I spot it almost immediately, tucked against the back of Cabin six, exactly where it belongs.

It seems Virgil is still here, and either he's walking the grounds without me this time, or he's still in his cabin.

Does he sleep in? I can't help but wonder, and I scour my brain for what we'd talked about yesterday.

Which…amounts to almost nothing of importance. He'd asked *me* about a lot of things, from my favorite food to my favorite color, yet when I'd turned the questions back at him, it felt like he'd looked for ways not to answer him. Like he wasn't interested in giving me the answer, even if I wanted to know.

"He'll be gone in a few days anyway," I mutter, hitting the gas to propel myself up the steep hill that takes me up to the highway. I'll never see him again, which is fine because despite what he said, he doesn't look like someone who does a lot of camping.

Not to mention he's a *reporter*. With the way he dresses and with how new his truck is, I'm sure he has a nice job up in Akron that keeps him busy.

And a girlfriend? The thought is an unwelcome one, and I shove it away as quickly as I can as I pull out onto the not-so-busy highway at the top of the hill. It's rarely busy here, given that we're in the middle of nowhere by the lake and Arkala is such a small town. I barely meet any cars on the highway, and the only thing of interest is the place that offers trail rides not too far from the campground.

I've never ridden a horse, though it's definitely on my bucket list. I *have* stopped by a few times to pick up pamphlets for the House, and while I've been there, the owner has let me pet and feed the horses a few treats while offering me a discount on trail rides.

"If you help me out sometimes, I'll let you ride for free," the older woman had informed me, her accent just as thick as Pat's. "I could use an extra hand 'round here. Dogs are welcome too, so long as they don't chase the horses."

"Oh, I really would," I assured her. "If I knew anything about horses or had ever been on one." That had been the end of it, mostly, though she had told me that I was welcome to come by and learn if I fancied doing so.

Maybe, eventually, I'd take her up on that.

Puffing out my cheeks, I glance in the mirror as I turn onto the road that will take me into the small town of Arkala. The best thing going for it is the big box store that doubles as a place to get groceries, though I avoid it and drive into the parking lot of a small strip mall instead. The *Arkala Mall* is old and run down, and I've seen stores come and go in the year and a half. I've been here so often that sometimes it feels like I have whiplash.

Only a few places are constants, including the bakery, a clothing store, and a furniture store that somehow manages to stay in business in a town that's best known for being near a campground and so close to the lake. I've only been in there once, and today I don't bother.

I'd much rather obtain coffee and pastries.

The owner and baker, a guy around my mother's age who wears a little gold nameplate that says *Adam*, beams at me as I walk inside with Argus on a leash and vested at my side. He's never given me an issue, and I doubt he ever will, but I'm always ready to paper cut someone with a small business card full of ADA regulations that I keep in a pouch on Argus's vest, just in case.

You never can be too certain how people will react to a service dog, after all. And I've been caught off guard often enough that maybe I've started to over-prep for the day someone gets past my *resting bitch face* to do it again.

"Good morning, Sloane," he greets, going to pluck a large plastic cup off a stack. "Do you want your regular coffee order?"

"I'd love that," I assure him, thrilled that he's not going to remark on how my coffee is probably about half cream. "And umm...can I get some bagels?" Gazing into the glass cases, I jab my finger at the jalapeño-cheddar bagels that look as fresh as they can be. "A dozen." I can freeze them, and that'll be my breakfast for the next week and a half easily, after I pick off the jalapeños, of course. I like a bit of residual spice from them having been on the bagel, but if I bite into one, I'll probably throw up.

"Sure, no problem." He moves to box up the bagels as I prowl around, still eyeing the rest of the food hungrily. If I could, I'd bring *all* of this back to my cabin. One of each thing so I could partake in a three-day feast and never leave except to lay next to the fire and *digest*.

But my wallet definitely can't handle all of that, so I point to the almond croissants on the end and add, "four of these, please?" Inwardly I tell myself that I'll freeze them, but I know that I'll probably eat two today and finish the other two off tomorrow.

"That it?" At my nod, Adam rings me up and hands me the boxes, my coffee coming right after.

"Oh. Crap." I hesitate. "Could I get two pup-cups? Vulc and Argus do such hard work, you know. I'd feel bad if they didn't get their sugar fix too."

That causes the brunette baker to snort, but he deftly fills two small espresso cups with whipped cream and sets them on top of the boxes that are in my arms. "Give them a big scratch for me, okay?" he says and comes around to push the door open for me as I go back out.

I consider dropping Argus's leash. He won't go anywhere, I

know, and it's been a long time since someone has made any kind of remark about him. But in the end, I keep it over my wrist as I walk to the car and only take it off when he jumps up into the back seat with Vulcan.

Of course, the two of them *devour* the pup-cups. The dreamy looks in their eyes remind me of a trance state, yet instead of being amusing, it makes me feel...strange. Trepidation churns in my stomach as I watch Vulcan, my lips pressed flat.

I know how he acts once someone has fed him. How could I not know when I've had him just as long as I've had Argus?

"Okay boys," I whisper when they're done, and I chuck the cups to the floor of the passenger side before reversing out of the parking lot. "Time to work, I guess. We have three days off, and we're going to earn sleeping in for all of them."

It's not until I'm back at the campground with my trunk unloaded of boxes that things go south.

My phone rings, and when I gaze at the number, I'm not surprised to see that it's a blocked caller.

Is it my stranger? I'm starting to wonder if he was the one who called me that first night so that he could sneak in, and that number had come up the exact same way as this.

But then, why would he be calling me during the day?

I sigh and hit the button to answer, the phone going to my ear a second later. "Hello?" I ask, ready for the sound of *nothing* yet again.

"Could you unblock my number?" My stepfather's voice is apologetic and sheepish. "*I hate having to use a different phone to call you. It's pretty shitty when all I want to do is apologize.*"

I don't say anything. My stomach *twists* violently, and I wonder if I'm going to throw up as I lean back against my car and stare out over the lake. How did he get my number?

I don't say anything because there's absolutely nothing to say to him. There never will be. I'm not interested in his apologies or whatever else he's trying to sell me.

"*Sloane?*" he prods. "*Hellooo? Did you hang up on me?*"

"Go to hell," I tell him simply, and before I can think to do any different, I hang up the phone and block the number. There's no other course of action to take. There's nothing else I want to do except scream as my pulse pounds in my veins and at my temples.

Why won't he just leave me alone?

I can't help the way my hands shake or the way I have to fight to not chuck my phone through the glass window of the House. I need to go home. I'm going to start a fire and shred some cardboard and eat all four croissants–

"I see my buddy has been relegated to the back seat." The rolling, soft chuckle catches me off guard, and I flinch, turning to stare at the speaker with open-mouthed surprise and I'm sure, a stricken look in my mismatched eyes.

Whatever Virgil is going to say dies on his lips when he sees my face, and a strange range of emotions crosses his face before he settles on a concerned frown. "You look like someone just ran over your cat," he informs me, stepping close enough that I can smell the sharp tinge of his cologne.

I don't take a step back, but I look down at his shoes instead of holding his gaze.

"It's not like that," I say, willing myself not to cry. My eyes find his hand that's shoved into the pocket of his jeans, and I focus on the snake tattoo that crosses his wrist.

My suspicions rear up again in my head, though they're pressed back by the gloom and dread my stepdad's call has cast on me. I want to say something. I want to confront Virgil and lay out why I think what I do.

But I don't have it in me.

"Then what's it like?" He doesn't move closer. He doesn't touch me, but I don't expect him to, and he doesn't do anything other than just *stand there*.

"Do you ever just wish someone would leave you alone? *Permanently*? Even if that means something really bad would happen to them?" The words slip out before I can stop them, and I reach up to press my palms to my eyes and sigh long and loud. "Sorry. That wasn't an appropriate question, huh?"

"I've wished that about a lot of people," Virgil chuckles, the sound full of amusement and wry humor. "Often, and with *feeling*. There's nothing wrong with hoping for someone to break their leg or their neck. It's only questionable if you help them along."

I'd help my stepdad along off a cliff.

I glance up at him, my eyes wide and rueful, and whatever he sees there makes his smile fade just a little. "Well, I'd never tell if you *did* do something like that."

"Do you promise?"

I shouldn't have said it. I should've kept my mouth shut or said *anything else*. And I shouldn't be standing here, staring him down, waiting for an answer that I don't know if I want.

Because if I'm right, if he is the man that's been paying me visits at night, then I'm not sure how to justify that in my brain or in the daylight.

Everything is always so different in the daylight.

Not to mention, if I let on that I think I know who he is, I'm not sure if his promise that he won't hurt me will hold when the sun is up.

It takes him a few seconds, but he grins and breaks the silence with a snort. "Yeah, Sloane," he says, taking a few steps away and heading back towards the path down to the lake. "If it makes you feel better, I absolutely *promise* you that I won't tell anyone should you help someone have an unfortunate accident. So long as it's not me."

Before I can think of anything to say, he's gone, disappearing towards the dock and leaving me with more unhealthy suspicions that I don't want to give myself the answers to.

10

When he doesn't show up by two a.m., it's pretty clear to me he's not coming.

Is it a coincidence? Maybe he tripped and fell into a wildcat and got *eaten* in the woods.

Or maybe it's because of what I said by my car. If I'm right, this is a pretty good indication of it. The fact that he's not here speaks volumes...maybe.

Or maybe he's just done with me.

That thought shouldn't bother me as much as it does. It shouldn't twist my heart and wring it like a soaked towel to think that the probable *murderer* doesn't want to come fuck me again.

I should be glad. I should be *thrilled* that he's left me alone and the only memory I have of him is a good one.

But I'm not. With a sigh, I get up and go to the kitchen, snagging a bottle of water before I head back. The dogs are on the couch again, *just in case*, but I've promised them that this is the last night I'll do this to them.

And the way things are going, it really feels like it will be.

God, that shouldn't be so disappointing. It shouldn't feel like someone is breaking up with me when I've only seen them twice.

Or, at least, only known them for a few days.

I untwist the cap of the water bottle as I sink back down in my bed, and it's not until I've tipped it back to take a long drink that I realize the screen on my window is gone again,

The realization makes me *choke*.

"Breathe, princess." My stranger pulls himself from the shadows of the far corner, having been able to hide there in his mostly dark clothing with my lights all off. Since I'm not expecting him this late, I hadn't kept the light on, but now that feels like it might have been a mistake.

He walks over to stand beside me, takes the water bottle from my hand, and sets it down on the bedside table as I gaze up at him with my lips slightly parted.

"I didn't think you were coming," I say, clearing my throat, so I don't cough. I try to keep the words casual as if I don't really care, but I don't think I succeed that well.

"Oh? Is that why you've been eagle eyeing your window all night?" The amusement is thick in his tone, and he reaches out to stroke his fingers over my hair until he can cup my chin and lift my face to his. "You *hoped* I'd come."

"Maybe I was scared you would, not hopeful?" I offer the words casually, but it's clear that I'm not being entirely truthful. His fingers thread into my hair, the feel of his leather gloves strange against my scalp, and *grips* hard enough that I gasp in surprise at the slight burn.

"Liar," the stranger purrs. "You're not good at it. Why even *try* when I can read you like a book?" He pushes me down onto the bed and then sits beside me. But instead of ripping off my pj's or demanding I strip, he instead catches my face once more. "Lie down on your back."

The way he says the words is...strange. Like he's not quite sure I'll do what he says this time.

"I won't hurt you," he reminds me. "Didn't I tell you that already?"

I shouldn't say anything. I should nod and either tell him to leave or lie down. But my traitor mouth doesn't know when to shut up, so instead, I look at the black eyes of his mask and ask, with barely any hesitation, "Do you promise?"

I swear he holds my gaze, though I can't see his eyes. But I don't look away, and finally, he scoffs and turns his head away. "Play with me for one more night, Sloane. You're trying to end this game so fast that I'm starting to think you don't like me."

It's as close as he can come to admitting I'm right without *actually* admitting I'm right.

"Maybe that's not my intention at all." I flop back onto the bed, bouncing a little from the force of it, and watch as he straddles my hips, still fully clothed. As always, he has the upper hand, and none of his skin is exposed, though my eyes linger at the sleeve of his jacket that obscures his wrist.

If I reach up and push it back, will I find the snake tattoo I'm sure is there?

"Then what *is* your intention, princess?" I wonder if calling me by my name was a mistake. A slip-up since he's only called me that once and it was a pretty serious thing before. He reaches one hand out and drags it up my body, pushing my loose shirt up so he can palm my breasts unobstructed.

"Maybe I just want to see your face from here on out."

He chuckles darkly. "Do you? Are you sure? Have you stopped to think that if I give you that much of myself that it'll mean I won't walk away? And do you really think you can handle *all* of me, princess?"

I don't know how to answer that. Especially when he reaches behind him and draws a long, wickedly sharp knife that gleams dully in what little light comes through the window.

I gasp, my muscles clenching, and my heart nearly stops at the sight of it.

"You fucking *promised–*"

"And I'm not about to break that promise. But if you want *all* of me. If you want me to *stay* for longer than I'd thought, then you can't just take me in small, measured doses. You'd better be prepared for every bit of me that I want you to *take*." His voice is low and husky, like the sight of the knife does more for him than it ever could for me. "You can say red, or you can say stop, and I'll leave. I promise."

I'm sure that it's problematic that his words uncurl something in me, putting me more at ease than I should be, given that I'm staring at the length of the *blade* between his fingers. But it does, and I nod my understanding as he lowers the blade to rest the tip between my breasts.

"If you must know..." He drags it downward lightly, the blade never once parting my flesh as I lay perfectly still under him. "I never intended to let things get this far. You're so difficult, especially with the dogs. Do you know how many extra steps I've taken to make sure they won't interrupt us?"

I don't move or answer. I can't when it feels like my voice is frozen in my throat.

"Close your eyes." I glance up at his mask again, not sure I can do that. "Close your eyes for me," he repeats, and I *force* myself to do what he asks, though my fingers twist in the sheets on either side of me and my body hums with tension and fear.

"I was just going to watch you. Or maybe kill you, though that idea went out the window *so* quickly. Once I saw you here, standing at your window and looking straight at me. Well..." I shiver as the tip of the blade circles my nipple, then moves to do the same to the other. "I thought for sure I'd frighten you enough to tell me to leave the first night. Princess, you really should've told me to leave. Look where you are now, hmm?" I love the tone of his voice and how it goads me as he trails the blade across my chest. "You're lying on your bed, practically naked, with a serial killer tracing shapes on your body with his *knife*. Does that seem very rational to you?"

Serial killer? My blood seems to cool in my veins, moving sluggishly as I try to process that. My lips part, I want to ask him something, but quick as a flash, the flat of his blade is against my lips, and he shushes me before I can even formulate a real question.

"Not tonight," he reprimands, dragging the blade down my face to stop at the base of my throat, where the point digs in just enough to make me feel it. "I'm going to let you sleep tonight," he goes on, sounding rueful at the confession. "I've kept you up for two nights in a row, and I can't expect for you to have any kind of real conversation if you're falling asleep on your feet. You're off for a few days, right? So you'll just be up here, making a fire or walking around the campground?"

I'm not sure how he knows my schedule. And while I guess he's just grasping at straws about my daily habits, he's pretty spot on.

Is he watching me during the day as well?

"But we'll have to talk, so it's unavoidable." The knife disappears, and I open one eye to see that his head is tilted to the side as he watches me. A soft scoff leaves him, and he cups my jaw in his hand, thumb running over my lips. "You can open your eyes," he informs me, and I open both of them to gaze up at the mask.

"Do I get to *speak* too?" I ask in an exaggerated stage whisper.

"Not with an attitude like that." He presses his thumb between my lips, apparently meaning what he says, and keeps my head back against the pillow as he sits up to loom over me, the mask garish in the darkness. "I'm going to leave," he reminds me. "Do you want to come before I go, or would you rather just go to sleep?"

His thumb leaves my mouth, resting on my lower lip. "Of course, I want to come," I whisper, my voice quieter than his.

"Don't look so excited. I'm not going to fuck you tonight, princess. Not when you need to sleep."

"Why?" He shoves his thumb back into my mouth as he reaches over me to rummage around in my drawer, and it takes me only a second to realize what he's looking for.

Sure enough, when he leans back and moves to sit between my thighs instead, he's holding my small bullet and the larger vibrator he'd fucked me with the first night.

"Because I fucking *said so*, princess. Don't get mouthy, or I'll tie you up and leave you here until morning with a vibrator in your pussy," he threatens, and there's nothing but serious promise in his voice.

The stranger shoves my legs apart, one hand on my thigh to keep it in place, while he uses the other hand to push my shorts to the side.

I'm expecting the buzz of a vibrator.

Not the feel of his fingers, ungloved, teasing my folds. I gasp at the new sensation, not sitting up or moving except to stare at the ceiling. The leather on my skin had been a deliciously new experience, but I want to feel *him*. Not just his cock, but his hands and his mouth.

I want to see the expressions he makes under that mask of his.

"Are you surprised?" It doesn't sound like a real question, and I don't think he wants an answer as he pushes two fingers into me and curls them, thumb on my clit. "You have to know how much I've wanted to touch you without the gloves."

"No, I...you're not exactly *easy* to read," I murmur, throwing an arm over my eyes.

"But you are." He continues to work me open on his fingers languidly, his touch causing heat to pool between my thighs. "And you shouldn't be reacting like this so *easily*, princess. It makes me think you're obsessed with my touch."

I might very well be.

"But you'd rather have my cock, wouldn't you?" He's not wrong. "*Wouldn't you?*"

"I want anything you give me."

He doesn't speak, as if my words have surprised him, and seconds later, my bullet replaces his thumb and hums to life on my clit. I buck my hips into him, unable to help myself, and I'm not surprised when he shoves me back to the bed before continuing.

"Don't run from me," the stranger purrs. "Otherwise, I might not fuck you with your other toy."

"Don't," I say and lick my lips before moving my arm to peer down at him. "I'd rather you use your fingers."

He pauses before letting out a sigh. "Careful," he warns, his voice dangerously soft. "You need to very be careful with your words. I'm going to think you mean them."

"I do."

"I'll make you regret them." He's silent as he teases me but doesn't exchange his fingers for the other vibrator as he works my body up and into a much *nicer* orgasm than the ones from the other two nights he's visited me.

I still cry out, however, and just barely manage not to whisper the name that I'm sure is his.

What if I *am* wrong? I don't think I am, but I don't want to ruin his game, even if I'm not.

He pulls his fingers away swiftly and crawls over me to tap them against my lower lip. "Clean off my fingers, princess," he purrs, leaning close enough that I can smell his cologne when I suck in a breath.

For me, it's the proverbial nail in the coffin.

But so is the snake tattoo on his hand that curls over the back of his palm. I stare up at the mask and open my mouth, allowing him to slide his fingers against my tongue as I clean my release off them while he watches.

He's not bothering to hide now.

And I know without a doubt who he is well enough that I want to reach up and pull the mask off his face.

But I don't.

Because he wants to continue this game for tonight, and I'm maybe, possibly, a little afraid that he'll be angry with me and not come back if I end it early.

At last, he pulls his fingers free and leans back, pulling the glove back over his hand before he stands up and walks towards the window.

"You could just use the front door," I point out, feeling drowsy all of a sudden. "Since you didn't get a chance to pet Vulcan today."

Virgil stops with his hand on the windowsill to look at me again, but I meet what I hope is his eyes as I drag my pillow under my cheek.

"*Careful*," he says again, then adds. "I'll see you in the morning, Sloane." And without another word, he's out of my window and blending in with the trees, as if he was never here at all.

And finally, I can let out the breath I was holding, the fear of him and the blade *whooshing* out of me all at once and soaking into the mattress below me.

    I'm still not sure I should've let him stay and less sure that I should've invited him back for more, but whenever he's here, I just can't do the right thing and use my *brain*, no matter how much I'm sure I should.

11

The eight a.m. knock on my door isn't the most welcome thing I've ever had happen to me this early. Even though my heart leaps in my chest and my insides *twist*, I can't help but wish he'd waited for another couple of hours until I'm properly awake.

Doesn't he know that business hours around here don't start until at least nine? Not in my cabin, anyway.

Vulcan barks from the couch and gets to his feet and is at the door before I can get there with his tail wagging uncertainly. He barks again, but I take my time, walking barefoot on the cold tile with my bagel half in one hand and the other free so I can pull open the door.

Maybe I shouldn't do this.

The thought rushes out the door faster than it formed, and my eyes land on Virgil.

But this Virgil is different from the one that I met at the House. Different from the one who asked me if I was all right on the deck and the one who asked me nonstop questions while we walked around picking up debris.

The Virgil in front of me stands almost perfectly still, his gold-flecked hazel eyes finding mine instantly. He stands with his hands in his pockets, hair perfectly just so, and he doesn't smile at me or move to make me more comfortable with a funny quip or a joke like I'm expecting.

He does, however, reach out and pet Vulcan as I take another bite of the bagel I'm holding.

"It's early," I observe, sure that I still sound like I only woke up recently.

"I could've woken you up," he points out. "But I let you fix breakfast first because I'm just that nice."

Oh. I take a moment to just look at him and chew on my slightly spicy and very cheesy bagel that's slathered in plain cream cheese.

"You could've just come in, and I don't know, watched TV?" I gesture to the television. "Not like Vulcan's going to chase you out, obviously." Before he can go on, I ask, because it's killing me not knowing, "What did you give him?"

Virgil doesn't answer at first. He grins, but the look isn't as friendly as it has been, and runs his hand over Vulcan's ears one more time. "Are you worried I was poisoning your dog?"

"No...." I feel a small lurch in my gut because that had never occurred to me until right now. "*Should I be?*" I'll kill him if he hurt Vulcan, psycho serial killer, or not.

"Of course not. I was giving him dog-safe peanut butter. I guess I'm just lucky that I picked it, even before you so helpfully told me what his favorite food is." He lets out a huff of air and stares at me, scrutinizing my features or maybe my expression. "Are you going to keep me outside all morning? I know you're pretty isolated, but people *are* walking along the road down there."

The knot uncurls slightly in my stomach, and I step back, gesturing for him to come inside. "Want a bagel too?" I ask as he looks around the small cabin appraisingly as if it's the first time he's seen it.

"This is *tiny*," he says, his gaze finding the couch where Argus lies watching him.

"It's just me," I point out, refusing to let myself feel self-conscious about my abode. "And the dogs. *Sorry* I wasn't expecting someone else. I would've cleaned up–"

He whirls around as I close the door with my elbow and steps towards me, one finger coming up to press against my lips. It's a good thing I don't have any half-chewed bagel in my mouth. I might've reflexively spat it at him.

"Stop," Virgil states, his voice carefully neutral. "You're scared of me, though I told you that I'm not going to hurt you. I *meant it*. You don't need to act so careless or prove a point."

As he speaks, Argus hops off the couch and calmly walks between us, using his bulk to push Virgil away a few steps.

The dark-haired man looks down, expression quizzical, and I pull away slightly to speak around the finger on my lips.

"He's tasking. He wants you to move."

"Why?" There's no frustration or malice in his voice, and he takes a step back and stops touching me when I say it, prompting Argus to sit between us and wag his tail as he stares up at me.

"Because I have a few problems, and people being in my space is one of them. I don't mind *now*, but he's trained to come between us if I don't let him know otherwise." I'm grateful to my dog, and I say the words quickly, in a perfunctory manner, like I'd explain them to a shopper in the grocery store.

Which I've had to do many, many times.

I expect Virgil to react like the majority of people I meet. Questions about my PTSD are common, along with comments of, *well you look fine*. Though, most people just want to know if they can pet Argus.

But he just looks down at my service dog, then back up at me, and says, "anything else I should know? I won't pet him unless you tell me I can. And if there's anything else–"

"No," I promise, cutting him off without meaning to. I don't expect him to be so *nice* about it. "You can pet him too. *Safe*, Argus." When I say the word, he turns away from me and gets to his feet, stretching as if he's showing off for the man who stands on the other side of him. "He'll task anyway if I need him. I should've realized he wouldn't like it if you–"

"Can I touch you now?" It's Virgil's turn to interrupt, though I can't help but catch the thread of amusement in his tone.

"Yeah."

He moves as soon as the word is out of my mouth and crowds me up against the door again, face only inches from mine. He's so close that I can feel the warmth of his breath on my parted lips, and his hand around the base of my throat might be the only thing keeping me upright.

"I *almost* kissed you last night," he purrs in that husky, sultry tone that I've grown addicted to in such a short amount of time. He presses his thigh between both of mine, trapping me in place. I nearly drop the bagel in my hand but manage to keep ahold of it as he lets out a soft exhale against my lips again. "Especially when you said you'd rather me use my fingers, princess. But you're so good at that, aren't you? Always knowing exactly what to say to me."

"I don't mean to," I whisper because I can't help it. "I don't set out to like–"

"I don't care if you mean to or not. It's a compliment. So don't change. I–"

Pounding on the door makes both of us jump, and my eyes

widen as I stare up at Virgil. I have no idea who it could be since Pat and Sam make it a rule to not bother me here, as it's supposed to be *my* place. And it's not like anyone else comes up here, for the most part, except my mom once in a while.

But I'm pretty sure the person banging on the door and sending reverberations through my spine is not my mother.

"Who's that?" Virgil asks, pale eyes flicking up to the green door above us.

"Fuck if I know."

He rolls his eyes and steps back, snagging the bagel half before it can go flying, and I whirl around to open the door, waiting for him to back into the kitchen so that he can't be seen from the door.

The person knocks again, and I yank the door open, half-expecting to see a Mormon or someone looking to sell me something I don't want, even though *I'm in a campground*. In reality, it's probably just a camper, that for some reason, has come to me for *something*.

It's not.

Of course, it's fucking none of those.

Anthony Murphy, stepdad of the year circa 2006 when he decided to kidnap me from school, throw me in the car, and almost *kill* me in a drunken fit after my mom filed for divorce, stands on my porch like he has any right in the world to be there.

He looks much worse than the last time I saw him, with bags under his eyes and hollow cheeks like he hasn't been eating enough. He's still tall enough to tower over me, and probably Virgil as well, and his skin is just as pasty-pale as it had been when I was a child. The biggest change is his hair, which has gone salt-and-pepper instead of remaining the shiny black that I remember.

My hand tightens on the door, and my heart rams into

my ribs. I suddenly feel like I'm eleven again, and nothing other than he and I exist as I stand there and stare up at him.

He terrifies me.

There's no way around it. His smile that's probably meant to be disarming does nothing except make my stomach roll like I might throw up, and the kind look in his eyes looks as genuine as a scorpion's promise.

For a long moment, I feel like I'm eleven again, and I realize for the first time that he has no intention of letting me go back home to my mom alive.

His smile widens as he stares at me, not noticing my expression or the way I want my heart to stop so I can stop being here.

"I figure it's harder to get rid of me when you can't just hang up the phone," he chuckles in his light baritone. "I just want to talk, Sloane. Though I admit, I wanted to come to see how you were doing, as well. I've seen pictures from Kate, but they don't do you justice."

Vulcan takes that moment to bark, his hackles up as he appears beside me to warn the man off like he would a coyote or small wildcat.

It surprises Anthony enough that he stumbles back a few steps, thankfully giving me the space that I need to suck in a breath that barely makes it to my constricted lungs.

Am I going to pass out? I try to breathe in again, but my chest hurts too much for me to do more than gasp for air.

Vulcan continues to bark, his teeth visible in his black muzzle, while Argus sits on the sofa and watches instead of joining in.

"Tell him to stop, Sloane," my stepfather snaps, clearly too afraid to come back on the porch. "This is ridiculous–" He takes a step forward, only for Vulcan to do the same, still putting on a good show of aggression that I doubt he'll follow up with a bite.

"*Leave*," I whisper, wishing I could do more than barely breathe out the word. "It's not a good time, it's..." I lick my dry lips. "It's *never* a good time, Anthony." With a grip on Vulcan's collar, I *drag* my dog back inside and slam the heavy door, locking it for good measure.

Resting my head against the cool wood, I wait, listening to his curses before I hear him get back into his car, the engine turning over a second later before it rolls down the driveway and back onto the main road.

My lungs burn, and I hope that with him gone, I can do more than gasp in oxygen. But when I try to take a deeper breath, my body rebels, and again I can barely get anything into my strangled lungs.

It doesn't occur to me that I've forgotten Virgil is in my house until I turn, only for him to push me against the door again with a careful emptiness on his face. "Who was that?" he demands. His strong hand once again at the base of my throat but without pressing.

I open my mouth, eyes wide, and try to answer, but nothing comes from my mouth other than a soft, breathy sound courtesy of my twisted-up vocal cords.

"I don't *share* what's—" It takes him that long to realize my profound issue and for him to see that Argus is trying to push past him to get to me. His eyes go down, then back to my face, and he transfers his grip to cup my cheek and lets Argus lick my hand fervently as if I don't know that I'm in the middle of a panic attack. "Tell me what you need," he orders, though any tightness or suspicion in his voice has been replaced with something that sounds remarkably like concern.

I, for one, want to *cry*. The fear of my stepfather being right outside burns, along with the humiliation of Virgil getting a front-row seat to my panic right *now* of all times. If I were him, I'd open the door and zip on out instead of standing here and dealing with me. I expect him to, and I won't fight him on it.

"I need–" I breathe in a sharper, shuddering breath, trying to remember how to appropriately get the oxygen I require. "I need to breathe. I can't breathe, I–" My shaking, clammy hands find his, and I try to communicate through that touch what I can't seem to do with my words.

"Okay." He nods like I've managed to answer the question and pulls me away from the door so that he can take me to my bedroom, which right now feels very small with both of us in it.

That or the walls are closing in as I all but hyperventilate in his arms.

It's not a request as he forces me to sit down on the bed, and his hand pushes me gently back until I'm lying down and staring up at him above me as he watches me with something that can't be the worry it appears to be.

The bed dips, heralding the arrival of Argus, who lays across my body and licks my face, managing to avoid Virgil as my dog does what he was trained to do and grounds me as best as he's able.

It works, though staring up at the man who I wanted to kiss about five minutes ago only serves to push further embarrassment through my body.

"You must think I'm so weird," I pant when I'm finally able to speak, and my lungs aren't constricted any longer.

"You don't know what I think, and you're not very good at reading me," Virgil points out with a small smile twisting the edge of his mouth upward. "Do you need anything?"

"A curtain of shame–"

"Hey." He touches my face with the back of his tattooed knuckles. "Stop, princess."

It's not fair when he calls me that because all I can focus on is him. I suck in a few breaths, both of us quiet before he speaks again.

"I *meant* it. You don't know what I think, and in this particular case, the only thing I am is *concerned*, all right? I want to make sure you're okay."

"It's not a one-off," I point out, in case it isn't clear.

"I figured that out, actually." He taps his temple and grins. "Once in a while, I'm able to put context clues together and see that you *probably* have a service dog for a reason."

"God, what does it say about you that *you* are more understanding than most people I meet?" I command Argus to *break,* and the dog gets up, though he goes to lie beside the bed and not far from me, just in case.

"I think you should worry for *them* more than me," he chuckles, watching as I pull my legs up under me to sit cross-legged in front of him. "And I hate to do this, but..." he lets out a breath.

My heart sinks. "But you're going to leave, check out early, and I'm never going to see you again?"

His gaze finds mine, brows rising. "*But,* I'm going to hold you to your word that we have a little talk. I'll be gentle with you. Well..." he shrugs his shoulders. "As gentle as I know how to be, which isn't saying much if you ask any of my friends."

"Do your friends know about your uh...hobbies?"

"My friends partake in their own hobbies that are just as bad but different flavored." He watches me as he says it, but I don't have it in me to be surprised or clutch my pearls.

"I'm happy that you have people to share your interests with," I say, barely thinking about the words before they leave my mouth. "Even if those interests are, uh–"

"Killing people?"

"I kind of like using the term *unaliving,* but that works too."

If I keep things flippant and chill, it's not so bad. Plus, it helps my panic ebb away, though I know this will leave me shaky and tired for the rest of the day.

And I need to call my mom; there's no more putting it off. I need to tell her he's probably broken a restraining order that *has* to be in place against this.

"We're going to be adults and say that I *kill* people." He shifts on the bed until he's sitting directly in front of me and mirroring my pose, his knees brushing mine. "And like I said before, you really should've told me to leave that first night."

I do a long, slow blink and try for a smirk. "You've told me that."

"I'm telling you again. Because maybe it wasn't clear enough the first time."

I digest the words, but they don't scare me. Nor do they particularly bother me. If anything, they're like a dare. A challenge, or maybe it's just him gloating. "What if I asked you to leave now?" I ask, wanting to know the answer. "I don't want you to, just to be clear. But what if I did?"

"Oh, *princess*." He reaches out to cup my jaw sweetly, urging me to lean towards him so he can reach up and swipe the pad of his other thumb over my lip. "Didn't I just tell you? That train has left the station. It's so far gone that neither of us could ever catch it. I guess I'd try. But I know myself. There is no *leaving* anymore."

My stomach does a little pirouette, and I part my lips just as he runs his thumb over them. "Does that scare you?" he adds in a soft voice.

"Should it?" I nip at his thumb, but he isn't *wrong*, exactly. Flickers of fear are present inside me, and I can't help the apprehension that isn't all due to the panic attack that hasn't completely left my body.

"It should terrify you. You should be running away from

me right now and going for help. You should find a camper, you should call the police. Tell them what I am. Tell them what I've done to you. Tell them what I *will* do to you if you don't."

I can't help but feel like it's a promise. The way my heart beats so loudly, I wonder if he can feel it in his fingers that are near my throat.

"What are you going to do to me?" I ask, wondering if I *should* ask or if I really want to know the answer."

It's the right question, or maybe the wrong one. His small, teasing grin goes wide, showing off white teeth and a predatory smile. "I'm going to wreck you. I'm going to *ruin* you. And the thing that you should be most afraid of?" He leans in until our lips are almost touching once more, and my breath hitches in my chest. "I'm going to keep you."

12

"What do you mean he showed up at your cabin?" My mother's voice has climbed a couple of octaves or so since we started talking, and I'm half-worried that she's going to pack up and *show up* before it's even midnight.

Which would be impressive since it's nearly ten at night and it would take her at least two hours to get here.

I sit back against the cloth camp chair and stare at the fire that I've built. Both dogs are on the other side of it, collapsed next to their food bowls with stuffed bellies that are full of food and the peanut butter that Virgil had snuck them before leaving.

"We'll talk later," he'd told me, standing up off the bed. "I need you in a good frame of mind." Then he'd just...left. Just breezed on out the front door as I'd watched and mourned the kiss that hadn't happened.

If anyone deserved to be killed today, it was my stepfather.

"He called me a couple of days ago," I explain, cringing when she makes a few choice comments about me not calling her earlier. "I know, I know. I'm sorry. He said Kate gave him my number." Her only response to that is a sharp intake of breath, and I can practically see her seething at my words.

"*He can't be there, Sloane,*" my mom promises me. "*If he shows up again, call the cops.*"

"Err..." I look off into the trees instinctively, as if Virgil is just going to appear.

If only it worked that way.

Sullenly I shift in my chair, my shorts riding up my hips as I fold my legs up under me and lean back. It doesn't seem like a good idea to call the cops with Virgil here. "I don't know, Mom. I don't want to make a scene."

"*You're not the one making a scene!*" She's irritated, but I know it's not with me. "*Are you off this week?*"

"I'm off tomorrow."

"*Can I come down to take you to lunch? I want to make sure you're okay. And discuss Anthony. He can't do that.*" She repeats the words like that'll make him just not show up again. "*I want to go over the rules of his release with you. And I'm going to have words with Kate in the morning.*"

I doubt those words will be 'have a blessed week.'

"Okay...yeah. If you want to?" Twigs snap behind me, prompting Vulcan to look up, his ears pricked, to stare off into the woods. Either it's nothing, or it's someone he knows.

And I'm sure there's only one person he likes that might be creeping up on me tonight.

"*Noon okay with you? Or will you still be asleep? I'm also bringing gifts for my grand-puppies.*" Her words make me snort, though half of my attention is fixed somewhere else entirely.

Like on who might be creeping up behind me. Prickles of anxiety run down my spine. I'd taken a long nap this afternoon, so I definitely feel better, but I don't feel one hundred percent just yet.

Not when I'm still afraid of my stepfather coming back to try to apologize, or whatever, again. I'm not sure how long the threat of Vulcan's fangs will last, but I hope that it's at least a week.

Or more, preferably.

"You spoil them so much," I snicker, closing my eyes as the breeze changes and more of the fire's warmth curls around my body. "Yeah, that's fine. If you have time and want to come down–"

"*I do*," Mom promises me firmly. "*No ifs, ands, or buts about it.*" I can't help but smile at the old saying.

"Okay. I'll see you at noon. Drive safe, Mom."

"*Sleep well.*" She hangs up without another word, and I rest the phone on my thigh for a second before I start to get up, wanting to turn and see if Virgil really is behind me somewhere.

But I don't get the chance. Leather gloves cup my face, holding me in place as their owner presses his nose to the top of my head and sighs.

"Don't get up. Not until I tell you to," Virgil purrs, running his hands down the side of my neck until he's gripping my shoulders. "I've been behind you for a few minutes now. I guess you knew since Vulcan was watching me."

"He's never going to let you sneak up on me again," I say, eliciting a chuckle from the man behind me.

"Is that a challenge, Sloan? Are you *daring* me to find a way to get to you without letting him know? And if I succeed, what exactly is my *prize*? Is it you?" One hand moves to cup my jaw, his thumb tracing my lips. "There are so many things I could do to you out here. And I bet you'd *let me* partake of every single one."

"Like what?" I can't help but whisper, tilting my head back to gaze up at him in the dark.

God, he looks so different in the firelight. In the daytime, even when he's not pretending to be someone he isn't, he still seems almost friendly. Approachable, attractive, and like someone that might help you if your car is broken down on the side of the road.

But at night, it's like he changes. His eyes are a darker gold, and nothing in them is polite or kind. He's playful and *dangerous*. He looks like he wants something that I'll be too afraid to give him or that he's daring me to try to get away from him.

A chuckle leaves him, reverberating in his chest. "I'm not going to sit here and tell you *all* of my plans for you. But one day, I'm going to make you *run*."

"My cardio sucks," I point out, keeping my tone light even as my stomach does a summersault.

"Oh, you're so funny, aren't you?" His grin grows like he's sharing my amusement. "You'd better hope your cardio is better than you think. I'm *nice*. I'll give you a few seconds, but wherever I catch you, you're getting thrown down and fucked like you deserve."

"What if I run that way?" I point to where the other campsites are, half-joking to see some measure of bewilderment on his face.

But I only get that fucking smirk.

"Then I'll assume it's because you want everyone who's here to *watch* me fuck you until you can't see or walk straight."

Oh. *Well*. That's not what I expected. He doesn't laugh or tell me that he's joking. Instead, he stands up and stretches.

It's only then that I realize he's in the black outfit from the nights he's come to see me, and the white mask is clipped to his belt.

The knife is there as well, in a holster on his thigh.

My insides twist, and I catch my breath as I watch him

work the knots loose from his neck before I dare to ask softly, "Were you doing something, umm...bad?"

His eyes open and find mine as the last few sticks in the fire that had been holding strong fall into a heap and release a puff of embers as their last attempt at life. "Nothing so bad that I can't trace your skin with this knife tonight," he promises, reaching out a hand to pull me to my feet.

I let him, snagging the jug of water that I use to dump over the remains of the fire. Then I walk over to put out the flames completely, mixing the water around with a stick so that I've found and snuffed any hint of an ember.

"Are you leaving?" I ask, setting the gallon of water on the ground. "For the night?"

"Do you want me to?"

"No." He follows me to the cabin, the dogs trailing after him, and I suck in a breath of air-conditioned, clean air before shivering in the colder room.

The door closes behind me, and he runs his fingers up my back before I turn to look at him over my shoulder.

"You...do that a lot," I say, immediately wishing I hadn't.

He quirks a brow and lays the mask on the table by the door. "Do what?"

"Touch me."

"Of course I do. Haven't you figured out why?" Two fingers become his splayed hand at the base of my spine, and a moment later, he hooks his fingers in the top of my denim shorts and pulls me back so that we're almost flush.

I shake my head at the question once I've discarded a few answers.

"To remind us both that you're mine."

Helpfully, that brings me to the crux of one of my concerns.

"Yeah, okay. So I'd like to talk about that, actually? If that's okay."

"You can talk to me about anything, Sloane." He uses his grip on my shorts to *drag* me into my room, but lets go so that I can sit on the bed, kick my flip-flops off, and drag my legs up under me again.

"You don't know me," I point out, sitting back and resting my weight on my hands. He doesn't immediately sit down but instead flips on the bedside light and turns off the larger one before placing his boots by the door and coming to sit on the bed as well. "You say that you won't leave. That I'm stuck with you, but how can you mean that when you don't know the first thing about me?"

He meets my eyes, tilts his head to the side, and says simply, "I know everything about you that I need to know. I've known since the first time I came in here a few nights ago that either you would make me leave or that I *never* would."

"You don't even know my favorite food. Or my mom's name. Or where I went to school. Or if we're compatible. Are we dating? Is that what this is?" It feels like something other than dating, but I don't know what to call it.

"We could call it dating," Virgil shrugs. "Is the problem that you don't know that stuff about me? You can ask me anything, and I'll answer."

I stop short, surprised by that. "*Anything?*" I repeat, calling him out on it.

He smiles slyly. "Anything."

He doesn't mean it.

"Have you really killed people?"

"Yeah, I have."

"How old were you when you first killed someone?"

"I was sixteen. My friend helped because he was kind of in love with me."

"Who was it?"

His smile never wavers. "My girlfriend's mom. She slept with my dad and broke up my parents' marriage."

Oh. Wow. That's...certainly not what I was expecting, and I stare at him, surprised.

"How did you kill her?" I don't know why I'm asking because I *don't need to know*.

"I stabbed her." He taps the knife on his thigh. "It's my preference to get up close and personal. I like to make a mess of things, and I like it when I can watch the life fade from someone's eyes." He pauses, eyes fixed on mine, and asks, "Does that bother you?"

Unfortunately for my sanity, my moral high ground, and my plausible deniability...it does not. "No. I don't think so? Do you still kill people?"

"I still kill people," he assures me. "But it's not so..." he tilts his head, thinking of the word he wants to use. "Indiscriminate as it was back then. I try to keep it to the people that maybe, probably deserve it. I don't want to go to jail because I'm predictable, after all. You would've been the exception to that, of course, if I killed you."

I don't think about the last part of his words. I'm obviously pretty grateful he did *not* kill me. "Are you worried about that? About going to jail?"

"Not at all. I've been doing this for a long time. I've never even come close to being caught. *Well*." He grimaces like he's thought of something unpleasant. "I'm *here* because I was a little....overzealous in reporting on the last crime that was all mine. It's hard not to get excited when you look at your own handiwork."

I don't know what to say to that, so I tuck it away for later. Or never. "What if it did bother me? What if I decide right now that you unaliving people–"

"Killing people, princess. We're not twelve."

"*Killing people*, then. What if I decide it bothers me? Would you leave?"

"No."

"Would you still kill people?"

His exhale is his answer, and he eyes me with lazy speculation. "I don't know," he admits. "I love to kill. I love how it feels to take someone else's life. But to stop you from trying to leave?" He rolls his shoulders in a shrug. "Maybe."

"But you've only known me for three days!" My voice raises, climbing in pitch, and I throw my hands up in the air reflexively. "Don't you see how *crazy* it is for you to say you'd try to give something up for *me*? Doesn't that seem *insane* to you?"

"Well, yeah." It doesn't seem to bother him very much, and that pulls me up short. "Of course, it's fucked up. *I'm* fucked up. I've been coming into your cabin every night to do fucked up things with you, and I have a literal list a mile long of all the things I'm *going* to do to you."

"You'll get bored after a while. I'm not that interesting, and I don't think I'll be joining you on your murder sprees," I point out lamely as my heart races at his words.

"I won't get bored of you."

"But how can you be *sure*?"

He reaches out and grabs the front of my shirt, dragging me to him until I'm half on his lap and straddling his knees. "I don't know, exactly. But the fact is, I *am* sure. I know myself well enough to know that much. I will *never* get bored of you or let you go. Those aren't just empty words."

He's going to kiss me. The fact dawns on me as I right myself as best I can on his lap, my hands on his shoulders as he loops his free arm around my waist. He's going to kiss me right here when we've been talking about him killing people and the fact that he's never going to let me go.

"I'm going to kiss you," he says, echoing my thoughts. "So take that time to decide how you want me to fuck you, princess. Because as soon as I'm done with your mouth, you have about four seconds before I rip off all of your clothes."

"It'll take me longer than four seconds to undress," I gasp as his mouth descends on mine, lips curving into a cruel smile.

"I know," he coos sweetly, mockingly. "I just want an excuse to be *rough* with you."

I can't say anything else. Not when his lips find mine for the first time, and he urges my lips open with his own. I give in instantly, allowing his tongue to invade my mouth and explore it like he's been waiting for this all day.

And maybe he has. Maybe I have, as well.

But it's not long before exploration turns to *devouring*. He pulls me more firmly against him, a fist in my hair, and his tongue recedes so that he can nip at my bottom lip until it stings.

Still, he doesn't pull away. He tugs and teases in earnest, teeth sinking into swollen flesh with a growl and my answering yelp. My body jerks at the sharp pain, but his tongue follows it as he hums praise against my lip and licks the small wound he's made, drawing my blood into his mouth before *finally* pulling away.

"Four seconds," Virgil reminds me. "And I've always had a bad habit of counting too fast."

13

Closing the cabin door behind me, I pause and inhale. My eyes fall onto Vulcan, who trots around the edge of the cabin with purpose and then I glance down at Argus.

It smells like I have a fire going, and the idea of one going in the fire pit *all night* makes my stomach clench uncomfortably.

That wouldn't have been possible, Sloane, I point out to myself silently. A fire would not have run all night on the *memory* of twigs, and the only way it could have is if the forest had caught fire. And as the trees still sway in the breeze above me, leaves rustling, I'm pretty sure that's off the table as well.

I don't wait to speculate further, there's no point. So I trudge towards the railing that blocks my cabin from the little campfire area and stop when I'm close enough to see what sits beyond.

A fire. In the fire pit.

But, perhaps more shocking, is Virgil. He sits on top of the picnic table, eyes fixed on his phone, and beside him in a flattened plastic grocery bag are s'mores ingredients and two shiny new long roasting sticks for them.

It's a good thing he's distracted because I just stand there like an idiot while Vulcan sniffs his shoes and try to get my brain to process what I'm seeing. My gaze flicks to the fire, and I note absently that it's well made, not just a pile of sticks and twigs thrown into the fire ring like he just dumped them there with abandon. There are even a few pre-cut logs in there I don't remember buying, meaning he really did come prepared, even though it's only eight-thirty in the morning.

When I look back at Virgil, I see that his eyes are fixed directly on my face, and I can't help but jump.

"Good morning sleepyhead," he teases, crooking a finger towards me.

"Good morning?" I can't help phrasing it like a question. I hadn't expected him to be here, first of all. Second, this is just all so...

Domestic, I suppose is the word that I'm looking for. *Domestic* like we're dating, and he knows me well enough to be aware that this is definitely something I'd enjoy and appreciate from him.

Hell, maybe stalking me has gleaned him more information than what I would've thought possible. If so, good for him, and congratulations on the dedication to his craft he's so clearly shown.

Or maybe he's just a really good guesser.

"You like s'mores, and you like fires." Neither is a question, and he beckons me over again until I'm sitting on the bench of the picnic table instead of up top like him. Almost immediately, he moves, sliding across the rough wood until he can bracket me with his legs and his knees are at shoulder level for me. I look up into his face questioningly, but Virgil just *grins* and doesn't give me any kind of answer.

"Yeah," I agree. "But do *you* like them?"

"I didn't really do this for *me*."

I stare at him, wanting an honest answer instead of the evasion that he's so good at giving me. Finally, Virgil sighs and lays his phone down, his hands coming forward so that he can stroke his fingers through my loose hair. "I like campfires," he admits. "I don't like s'mores that much. Though I'm sure if you put a marshmallow in your mouth right now, I'd be happy to fight you for it."

I snort and glance at the bag beside his thigh. "I think there's enough that we don't have to go at it gladiator style," I inform him dryly, leaning against the wood and the V of his legs. "I'm just...surprised. I would've thought you had better things to do than wait until I wake up with a fire and s'mores all ready to go."

"I don't have anything better to do."

"Yeah. I...I got that." It's so *strange* to be sitting here like we've been *dating*. Like he knows me and everything about me, and that we're closer than near-strangers.

Though it doesn't quite *feel* like we've only known each other for a few days. Not with how comfortably I melt against him.

Which is definitely problematic, given he's a *serial killer,* and I don't see myself unaliving anyone anytime soon.

Then again, all things are possible through good sex and kink, as the saying maybe goes. So who am I to say what I will and won't do in the future if he keeps coming into my cabin and *railing* me at night?

"Tell me something about you?" It bothers me slightly that he knows more about me than I do about him, and if this is going to be a *thing*, I want to rectify it.

"Like what, princess?" I love the way he says the nickname and the way it feels slightly inappropriate during the daylight.

"Like..." I search my brain for something and scramble not to come up blank. "What's your favorite color?"

"Magenta."

"Weirdly specific, but okay." I suck in a breath. "Favorite animal?"

"Dogs."

"Favorite food?"

"Chili dogs."

"Really?"

His grin widens, and he ruffles my hair. "Yes, *really*. Why is that so surprising when I'm pretty sure *your* favorite food is marshmallows?"

He's not wrong.

"I don't know. Chili dog is just so random. I would've thought you were very new-age Hannibal Lector and enjoy only the finest steak and red wine to remind you of...you know." I trail off, my words becoming a whisper.

"Of the blood of my many victims that I've killed in oh-so creative ways?"

"Yeah. I just didn't want to say that out loud." His nails scratch my scalp, and I sigh, unable to stop myself from shivering just a little.

"Why? There's no one up here to hear us. Unless the dogs are going to tell." His words prompt me to look up, and I see that both dogs are sniffing around the edge of the woods, looking appropriately entertained. "You can ask me about it if you want. About *anything*. I won't hide anything from you."

"What if you scare me away?"

"Oh, Sloane. I've *tried* to scare you away." He tugs on my hair. "I've tried the best I know how. Outside of *actually* hurting you, I suppose. At this point, I'm going to assume you're not afraid of anything."

That's absolutely a lie. My own PTSD *puts* the lie to his

words, and I frown up at him ruefully. "That's totally not true and you know it," I remark quietly. "I'm *terrified* of my stepdad."

"The guy who was here yesterday?" Virgil's eyes darken. "Why?"

"I thought this was when *you* tell me shit about yourself?"

He sighs and slides his hands down my shoulders, leaning over me until his body forms a very comforting, very restrictive cage around me. His arms wrap around my shoulders, then he pulls back to sit up once more. "I'll tell you whatever you want to know. But *I* want to know what he *did* to you."

I'm not sure how I feel about the growly, possessive tone.

"It was a long time before I met you," I point out, trying to quiet my racing heart.

"Obviously, or he'd be dead right now." I don't know how to process the empty, blunt words, so I don't bother trying.

"He kidnapped me," I say finally, letting out a breath I hadn't known I was holding.

Virgil sits up and picks up the s'mores ingredients, pulling things open and setting them onto plates as I talk.

"When I was eleven, my mom decided she'd had enough of him. He was emotionally and verbally abusive towards both of us. More her than me, since he said I was the daughter he'd always wanted and *normally* treated me like it." I reach my hand up for one of the sticks, but Virgil keeps it out of my reach as he moves to sit down on the bench beside me, his thigh and shoulder pressed to mine. I watch as he sticks the marshmallow over the fire, not quite in it, and patiently just *waits*.

When he catches my eyes on him, he smirks. "Did you think I was going to just stick it in the flames?"

"Absolutely," I admit without pause.

"I told you, one of my best friends *loves* camping. His mom owned a campground, and there were summer camps there every year at the lake. He went *every year* and he's insane about how we're supposed to toast marshmallows."

"Even now?"

"*Especially* now." His smile is teasing, and he leans over to kiss my cheek. "I'll toast your marshmallow."

"That sounds kind of kinky."

"But *you* need to tell me what happened." His tone turns firm as he says it, and I can't help scrunching my nose at his words.

"*Thanks*," I mutter and let out a breath through my nose. "Yeah, so I'm not going to drag it out. He picked me up from school when Mom said she was divorcing him and told me he was going to take me home early. Instead, he drove me out of state and went *crazy*. He was drinking, too. And told me that Mom would have to take him back since he had me. Then said I'd be better off dead so that I wouldn't feel the same kind of heartbreak he felt." I say it quickly, perfunctorily as though it happened to some other chubby eleven-year-old with wild auburn curls instead of the one sitting beside Virgil.

"So Mom got the police involved, obviously. It took them the better part of a day to track him down to this old motel his friend owned. He had a knife and threatened to kill me. He'd almost done it before having a bit of a *fit*." I grip the neckline of my tee and yank it down, showing him the small scar between my collarbones. "And now I have PTSD and a dog trained to sock me in the face if I don't listen to him and *sit down* when I'm starting to freak out."

Virgil doesn't reply for a few seconds. He removes the properly toasted marshmallow from the fire and sets it onto the graham cracker and chocolate, puts the other cracker down on top of it, and then turns to wrap me in a hug and bury his face against my hair.

"So don't take this the wrong way, but I could kill him for

you," he murmurs, pulling me against him more thoroughly. "You could watch, I could video it, or you can help. *Or*, we can just not talk about it."

I snort against his t-shirt. "You can't kill my stepdad."

"Why?"

"Because that's..." I let out a breath and turn to press my mouth against the side of his neck to distract him. I can't really think of a reason that he *shouldn't* kill Anthony, frankly, which should probably be troubling.

He chuckles, his arm going lower around my waist as I kiss from his neck to his jaw. "Are you trying to *distract* me?" he teases, turning so he can kiss me fully when my lips are close to his.

"No, never," I lie. "I was just struck by an *urge*."

"I know that urge," he replies with fake enthusiasm. "It's the same *urge* I get when I look at you and can't help thinking how good you look on your knees, waiting for my cock."

"It's eight-thirty in the morning."

"And I haven't fucked you yet. I *know*, it's been forever. But I did make you a s'more?" He holds it up in front of my face, prompting a laugh to escape my lips.

"You did," I say, nodding sagely and plucking it from his fingers. "You *so* did. How will I ever repay you?" I take a bite and chew, swallowing it moments before Virgil's lips find mine again.

"Maybe by letting me have a taste," he purrs, his tongue sweeping over my bottom lip before he puts his free hand in my hair and holds me in place just so he can explore my mouth and lick up every hint of sweetness there.

When he pulls away, I feel hotter than I should, and I suck in a breath to compose myself. "Good enough for you?"

He hums thoughtfully. "No. Not enough chocolate. Take another bite, let me taste it again."

"You could just *eat it* yourself."

"But *Sloane*," he gazes at me, all puppy-dog eyes and earnestness. "Don't you know that it tastes so much better when it's from your mouth?"

The second time my mom knocks on the door, calling out my name, I open it just as I've pulled my shirt on and *beam* at her, hoping my hair doesn't look as bad as I think it does. I definitely hadn't expected her a half-hour early, and I'm amazed that she doesn't remark on how I look or how red my face probably is.

God, I hope she hadn't heard my *shriek* when she'd gotten out of the car. Hopefully, she'd still been safely behind the wheel when Virgil had bit down on my still-throbbing shoulder and come inside of me.

It's hard not to glance behind me towards my bedroom, where he's currently getting dressed.

"Hey Mom," I say, smiling and stepping forward to throw my arms around her shoulders. She's just as tall as I am, with the same build, but her hair is straight and long, and her eyes are both blue instead of my heterochromia.

"Sloane," she murmurs and squeezes me in a tighter embrace than is strictly necessary. "Are you okay? I was scared you'd be a wreck after that *asshole* came to see you. Fuck him, by the way. I'm in touch with our lawyer and he's reporting this to the courts and his parole officer. It's *not* okay for him...to...."

She trails off, her eyes narrowing in confusion. I don't need to turn around. My hearing is fine, and I know that Virgil has come out of my bedroom and gone into the kitchen like he lives here too.

He'd better have a shirt on since my mother is here.

"Who is that?" she asks, craning around me to get a better look.

"That…is my boyfriend," I say impulsively, cringing internally. I'm not sure *he'd* want me to use that word precisely. And I'm not sure we *are* dating. Is that even the proper word for what we're doing?

It definitely doesn't seem like it.

"His name's Virgil."

"Boyfriend?" She looks at me again. "You haven't told me about a *boyfriend*."

Well, Mom, I don't say, *that's because I've only known him for a little less than a week, ever since he started stalking me and decided I'm too great to kill. So wonderful job in raising me!*

She'd have a heart attack if I tried to tell her even *half* of that.

A sigh behind me lets me know that Virgil is back, and from over my shoulder, I can see him slightly wave to my mother in greeting. "Hello." His voice is higher and more amicable than usual. With a shock, I realize it was the voice he used when he checked in to the campground.

And he doesn't use it around me anymore.

"You didn't tell her about me?" Virgil puts a hand over his thankfully *clothed* chest, just above his heart, like he's offended. "Are we not *serious*, Sloane?" He's overtly teasing enough that my Mom knows he's joking as well, and I scoff wryly at him.

"You just haven't come up," I tell him, pushing at his hand. "Mom, I have a boyfriend. Maybe it's a little late, and I should've told you sooner. But." I gesture theatrically to him with both hands. "He's cool and this is him."

My mom looks him over appraisingly as if she's a bloodhound and can smell my lies. "How do my grand puppies feel about him?" she asks finally, switching her gaze back to me.

"Oh, Vulcan *loves* him," I assure her, leaving out that it's because he sat in the woods with peanut butter to win him over before breaking into my room and fucking me until I lay boneless on the bed.

She probably doesn't need to know that, after all.

"Really?" She glances back at Virgil, still skeptical. "What do you do for a living?"

"You are not about to play twenty questions with-"

"I'm a reporter," Virgil answers smoothly.

"Do you own a house?"

"I have a condo in Akron."

"How serious are you about Sloane?"

He looks at me, his gaze softening the perfect amount. He's *practiced* at this, I realize. He knows exactly what to show my mother to make her believe we're together.

How terrifying.

"I'm *very* serious about your daughter. I was here when your ex-husband showed up, and I wish I'd done more to preserve Sloane's peace of mind. In the future, I hope to be better. I'm...still learning how to react when Argus is tasking and what I need to do for her in those cases when she's struggling."

Damn, he's good. It's uncanny, and I make a mental note to ask him about it later.

His words appease my mother, and her metaphorical hackles go down. She sighs and looks him over, begrudging fondness already blooming on her face.

He's so good it's *eerie*.

"Then it's nice to meet you. I'm Emma Walker." She holds her hand out, and he shakes it respectfully.

"It's nice to meet you too, Ms. Walker. Like your daughter said, I'm Virgil Olsen." His voice remains pleasant and maybe a little *boyish*. "I have to go for a while..." he leans over and kisses my temple affectionately. "But have a good afternoon, ladies." Quietly he sidles out, bidding goodbye to both of us again before walking down the hill to where his truck is parked farther down.

How had I not noticed it there earlier? Had he parked it away from my driveway *specifically* to surprise me this morning?

"He's sweet." My mother watches him go, her tone still holding a hint of suspicion. "But that was unexpected. Is there something you aren't telling me?" When I look at her, I find her gaze back on mine, and I smile wryly.

"Look, it's just been...*intense* with him. We haven't known each other terribly long."

"But you're serious about him?"

"Deadly." I almost flinch when I say it, and I'm glad Virgil can't hear how corny the confession is. I'm such an idiot.

"We'll talk about it. But first..." she reaches a hand up to show me the pet boutique bag that dangles there, "let me in so I can love on my puppies. They *miss* me, you know."

"Uh, they miss your luxury treats and all of the other *insane* things you get them," I laugh, stepping back so she can come inside.

The dogs, who had been crowding me while we spoke, swarm her with wagging tails and lolling tongues, thrilled to see their 'grandma' who's come to them bearing gifts as any proper grandparent should.

Hopefully, by the time she's done, she'll be too focused on wanting to talk about Anthony to worry or ask anything further about Virgil.

Because I'm running out of things to tell her, and I won't know where to go from there.

14

There he is again.

It's good luck that I have a lot of different hiding places in the campground. And while I know my mother wants to know Anthony's every move, I've texted her four times today, telling her that he's hanging around, clearly looking for me.

Already he's been to the House, presumably to talk to Pat and Sam about my whereabouts since he most certainly did not find me back at the *locked* cabin. But they know not to tell him either.

Vulcan whines at my side, shifting as I sit on the swing and watch Anthony's SUV go by again. Through the trees and up a hill beside the more private campsites, I know there's very little chance he's going to find me up here, but the dogs are leashed anyway. I don't need them bounding down and giving away my position or ending up on the road to get hit.

Call me paranoid, but I don't want anything to happen to any of us. And I don't trust my stepfather to *not* run over my dogs for spite.

Footsteps crunch on the gravel behind me, and I don't need to look up to know that it's Virgil that wraps his hands on the chains of the swing and pushes me forward slightly, my sneakers skimming the rock under me.

"Offer still stands," he tells me, his voice mild. Vulcan licks his hand, just visible at the corner of my eye, and pants at him with his eyes wide and begging. He wants Virgil's attention almost as much as I do, though it's in a very different way that my dog craves my *boyfriend*.

What a strange thing to say. Or rather, think. He hasn't said anything about my use of the word, though I haven't gotten to talk to him much since my mom went home late last night, promising she'd be careful and reminding me that she loves to drive at night.

Which is definitely a trait I did not acquire from her.

"The offer to kill my stepdad?" I ask almost gloomily, using the swing's momentum to stop myself and lean against him. I gaze up at Virgil, who watches me with a carefully neutral expression, though when I quirk a brow at him, I can see a smile flicking at the corner of his lips.

"Yeah."

"That seems suspicious. I'm worried you'll get caught."

"Shouldn't you be telling me to *stop*? Reminding me of my humanity or my morality?" He's joking, clearly. Teasing me like I've forgotten what he is or who I've been letting into my cabin day and night.

"Uh, no. He's a piece of crap. But..." I let out a heavy sigh and lift my feet up so that the swing slants forward once more, and I'm able to skim the gravel with the toes of my shoes. "You can't just go around killing people for being kind of crappy."

"He's more than kind of crappy, and I assure you that I can." His arms move so he can drape them over my shoulders, and both of us watch him go along the main drive of the campground once more. "Have you not told your mom about him being here? I thought she'd been rather adamant about calling the cops if he returned."

My eyes narrow and I glance up at him. "That was a private conversation we had after you left," I point out, my voice mild. I'm not upset, obviously. Stalking is just part of his thing, and I'm too emotionally tired by the yo-yoing of Anthony in the campground to do more than point it out.

"I listened for a while," Virgil shrugs. "Sue me. It's a hobby, princess. If you have an issue with me listening, then I'm fine discussing–"

"I don't mind," I break in. "Not over this, anyway. If you want to listen to me bitch about my shitty stepdad, then who am I to stop you–" I break off when Anthony's truck slows near the entrance of the road that leads up the hill towards our spot. If he starts to come up here, I'll have to find somewhere to hide.

I can't face him today. I can't tell him to go away again.

"So, are we expecting the police to show up anytime soon?" Virgil prods, hands going to my shoulders.

"Guess not. Mom said she's called, and they were going to send out a non-emergency vehicle or something." I say the words as flippantly as I can, all the while pretending I haven't been looking at the entrance of the campground and praying that someone would show up to get rid of him.

He goes by the ramp, and I let out a heavy sigh of relief.

"Sloane..." Virgil's fingers stroke over my hair and comb through it softly. "He's going to come up here eventually. What's your plan for that? Do you have one?"

A wry smile curves on my lips. "Oh, I absolutely have one. A good one, too."

"Care to share, princess?"

"I'm going to launch myself into the woods and hide."

"I..." He trails off and sighs, fingers picking through sections of my auburn hair. "That's not really a plan."

"It's the best one I have."

He's quiet for a few moments, and we watch Anthony's truck circle the campground around the tents, where he slows like I might be hiding among them or behind a water fountain.

Will he get out a spotlight next and try to catch my eyes to paralyze me like a deer?

"I don't get what he wants," I hiss, my shoulders tight. "Like, I've made it clear that I don't want him here. I'm not interested in him trying to make amends. *I don't want to make amends.*" My voice rises until I sound almost hysterical. "Why is he still looking for me? How is he *allowed* to be here?" I hate the way I sound and the way my heart pounds in my throat.

"I can't really answer that." Virgil doesn't seem too invested in trying, but that's fair. He has no reason to know either. "But I *can* offer a different solution if you'll let me."

I huff, my shoulders falling, and shake my head. "You can't kill him and throw his body in the lake. Someone will find him."

"That's amateur of you, Sloane." he sounds a little reproachful when he says it. "If you're going to start coming up with murder plans, we'll have to talk about how well they'd work and what your chances of getting away with them are."

"It was a joke."

"Not when you think I'd really do it." He cups my chin in his hand, thumb stroking over my bottom lip. "Stop being a brat with me for a minute and listen." It isn't a request. I'm not surprised. "I need to run back to my home in Akron," he tells me, though it's hard to focus on anything other than the weight of his thumb against the seam of my mouth. I want him to push his thumb inside and tease my tongue.

He's good at that, after all.

"So you're leaving for a little while?" My stomach clenches when I say it, though I try to keep my voice casual like it doesn't bother me. I'm not sure how this is a suggestion, either.

"Let me take you with me," he urges. "You and the dogs. Let me throw you over my shoulder and steal you away to my house. If it makes you feel better, I don't mind pinning you down and restraining you. You'd like that." He doesn't ask, just assumes, but he's probably right. "We'll make it feel so real."

"Who are you trying to convince? Your *willing* victim? I don't think you need to sell me on that, Virgil. Besides, I can't. I only have two more days off. I really can't."

"We'll be back in two days," Virgil assures me. "Or one. Whatever you want. I'll make sure to get you back in time for work, Sloane."

"That doesn't sound very abductor-ish of you."

"What can I say? I'm going soft." He wraps his arms around my shoulders again and turns to kiss the side of my throat. "Don't say no," he breathes against my skin. "What's the harm? I'll take you on a few dates, we'll camp out in my condo. We'll have *fun,* and I'll let you blast the AC like you do in your cabin."

"I don't blast the AC."

"Yeah, you do. Sometimes I think you're seeing when it'll *snow* in there." He nips my shoulder, and I sigh to cover up a whimper.

"You won't kill me." It's not a question, but I still can't help the touch of fear the snakes through my nerves.

"I won't kill you," he assures me, the question seeming to

not bother him. Almost as if he expects me to ask, even though I've done so at least sixteen times before. "I will *never* kill you or harm you. And I'll remind you of that anytime you need me to. But I will take you away from this when it becomes too much."

"Even if I'm kicking and screaming?"

"That's not the threat you think it is." A small part of me wants to tell him to *make me* go. The idea thrills me and makes my breath catch in my throat as I imagine him being unnecessarily rough with me.

That is, until Anthony's SUV drives by again, and again he slows down by the ramp that leads up here.

"Okay," I say, getting to my feet and handing Vulcan's leash over to Virgil when he puts his hand out for it in question. "Don't let him pull you down the hill. And what's the plan? I don't see us walking back to the cabin without him seeing us."

"It's a straight shot from over there, down the hill, to your back window." The explanation catches me off guard, and I glance sharply at the dark-haired, sinfully sexy man that stands behind me with one hand in his pocket and a completely at ease pose. His expression remains concerned and friendly, even as I scrutinize him with narrowed eyes.

"What?" I ask, finally. "How do you know that?"

"How do you *think*?" He crooks a finger at me, and I follow him, walking to the place he pointed out and following him off the road as the sound of a car gets steadily closer.

Thankfully, by the time Anthony is close enough that he would've seen me on the swing, we're deep in the woods and obscured by the trees enough that there's no way he'll know anyone's back here, let alone me.

The whole time I spend packing up my backpack with everything I'll need for a couple of days, I'm terrified. I'm sure that at any moment, Anthony is going to come back and that he'll realize I'm here. Not to mention that I'm here *alone* since Virgil had to go get his truck for us to escape in.

God, I hope he doesn't do anything violent to my stepfather.

Why not? My brain demands, the words echoing around in my head unbidden. *Why would it be such a bad thing if he killed Anthony?*

My hands slow, though I don't mean for them to. My packing crawls to a turtle's pace, and I bite my bottom lip hard enough for it to sting. It's wrong to ask Virgil to end my problems with a knife; worse still that the thought of him doing it doesn't elicit anything other than cold hope.

After all, I can't control my new boyfriend. If he does something, then what can I do other than make sure that neither of us pays for it?

Anthony's death would be a *shame*.

A tragedy of the least-epic proportions.

An engine outside grabs my attention, and Vulcan gives a short, loud bark to let me know that someone is definitely here.

It doesn't *sound* like Anthony.

But both of them drive big enough vehicles that I don't know if I could tell them apart with any kind of accuracy. Especially now, when I'm freaking out a little bit.

A door closes, and footsteps sound on the wood of my porch outside. Vulcan waits, whining, and I take that as a good sign as my blood rushes in my veins. *What if it's not Virgil?* My brain whispers treacherously. *Did you lock the door? Maybe you didn't. Maybe you should–*

The door pushes open, my heart nearly stopping, until I see Virgil stride in, his face calculating and expressionless.

"Time to go," he says, picking up the dogs' bag and my

pillow, though he glances at the latter with confusion and a slowly rising brow.

"I always take a pillow," I shrug, a little bit self-conscious.

"I *have* pillows, Sloane."

"Well, maybe I won't like any of them."

He opens his mouth, closes it, and grins. "Okay," he says, and without the argument I'm expecting, he takes the things to his truck and puts them in the back. "Can I load up Vulcan?" he calls back, *thrilling* me with the sheer fact that he's always willing to ask first instead of assuming.

"Yeah!" I zip up my backpack, wondering if what I've packed is good enough for what he wants to do or not do. "I'm ready." With a last, quick plea to whatever's out there that everything will work out, I follow him out the door and toss the backpack in his truck, then let Argus jump up as well.

"You have everything?" He closes the back door on his side and opens the driver's door to lean on the seat and look at me, where I rest my arms on the passenger side.

"I..." I suck in a breath, and I can hear the sound of another approaching car.

Our time might be up.

Virgil seems to have the same idea because he glances at the road behind him, then at me.

"Yeah," I say and dart back to the door to lock it. I'm grateful I don't drop the keys or bash my face on the door like I would if this was an actual scary movie.

In a flash, I'm at the truck and in the front seat, closing the door and dropping my keys in the console as Virgil puts the truck in drive and heads down the driveway.

Again we're *just* lucky enough. My stepfather's SUV rounds the bend too late to see where we've come from, and I duck down under the window as best I can, hoping that he doesn't see enough of me to know who I am.

Virgil, on the other hand, waves and smiles savagely at my stepfather, his expression not fading when he looks at me and says, with feeling, "God, you should really just let me kill him and get it over with."

15

It's been at least a year and a half since I've been in Akron, Ohio. Maybe a little bit longer, since I'm pretty sure the last time I was here was when I'd had my appendix out and mom had offered for me to stay in the house, to be able to help me with everything.

It hasn't changed much, though I do like looking at the city from Virgil's condo on the seventh floor of his building. The railing is stable and sturdy, easy to lean on, and solid enough that I know the dogs aren't going to go through it.

Not that they're out here with me. Argus is sleeping on the sofa, tail tucked over his eyes as he takes a much-deserved nap. He hadn't slept at all on the drive up here like Vulcan had, and I'm half-wondering if he'll sleep until noon tomorrow.

Vulcan, on the other hand, is busy trying to *eat* Virgil. Or, at least, that's kind of what it looks like if I turn away from the view to watch.

In reality, he and my stalker-boyfriend are playing tug-of-war with an old shirt that Virgil had produced, and I know for a fact Vulcan has dragged him across the floor at least once.

It's amazing how well he does with dogs—my dogs, to be exact. While Argus likes him in an acquaintance kind of way, Vulcan is *all over* him like Virgil is the greatest thing since sliced bread.

Part of it, of course, is the peanut butter. But a big part of it is just *Virgil*

I'm not jealous, but I am surprised.

The door behind me slides open, and I don't turn around as Virgil wraps his arms around my waist and rests his chin on my shoulder. "Hi," he purrs sweetly into my ear, kissing my jaw a moment later.

I hum thoughtfully, my eyes finally slanting to the side so I can just barely see him. "You've kidnapped me back to your condo," I remind him, the statement only partially false. Consensually kidnapped, sure. "So what now?"

"Umm, now I tie you up, never let you leave, and sway you to the dark side?" he offers, brows raising when I turn to look at him fully. "That's really how these things work, Sloane. I thought you knew that by now."

My stomach does little summersaults, and I study his face. "I wouldn't know," I say finally. "My last experience with being kidnapped was a lot less enjoyable than this one."

"Yeah, maybe let's not compare the two," Virgil suggests with a snort. "Anyway. I thought you'd maybe want to go get dinner? I definitely don't have any food here in the condo, so we're either going out or calling–"

He breaks off when his phone rings in the back pocket of his jeans and waits.

I guess a normal person would actually reach into their pocket and either answer or just reject the call. But not Virgil. He just *stands there* like nothing's happening and watches my face with his gold-flecked hazel eyes.

Finally, it stops, and Virgil opens his mouth again, only for the phone to pick up its ringing once more.

This time Virgil sighs and reaches into his pocket, palming his phone and bringing it to his ear as he answers. "What?" He doesn't sound thrilled and maybe a little grumpy, but I'm pretty sure there's an undertone of amusement like the caller is someone he can't be mad at for long.

He waits, listening, his eyes still on mine as he does. "I'm busy," he says at last, a half-smile coming to his lips. "Yeah, with *Sloane*." He says my name like he's trying to get the point across. Though I'm not sure what that point is. He frowns, lips flat, and blinks as he studies me. "I'm not sure," he sighs.

If only I could hear the other side of this conversation.

"Seriously, I'm not sure if–*yes*, I could ask her, Wren. But maybe *I* don't want to see your face today."

Wren must be a person, I assume. One of his friends, maybe?

One of his homicidal, serial killer friends?

Virgil sighs through his nose and looks away, only to put the phone on speaker and hold it between us. "My *best friends* want to go out for dinner tonight," he says, loud enough to be obnoxious. "They apparently want to rub my face in something they think I've done, and they want to give you a good laugh."

I stare at him, nonplussed, my hands flexing on the railing. *Your friends know about me?* I want to ask the question that's right on my lips, but instead, I just wait for the question that I hope is coming.

What do they know about me? I can't help but wonder if they know that he'd once thought about killing me. Or about how he broke into my cabin, and I didn't have the good sense to kick him right back out.

Though in my defense, the sex is great and would be a real loss if I had told him to leave.

"*And we want to meet you,*" the tinny voice on the other end of the phone adds. "*He's leaving that out on purpose.*"

"*And we like dogs?*" A different, quieter voice says. "*We won't hurt your boyfriend.*"

They know about Argus?

"*Speak for yourself. You aren't the one getting ripped apart by Miss Maneater herself for his shit,*" the first is quick to say.

"Are you asking me if I want to go?" I look at Virgil, eyes a little wide, and he just stares flatly back at me. "It's probably not *my* decision–"

"*Oh, it definitely is,*" one of his friends assures me. "*Don't let him act like he can just boss you around. If you want to go somewhere, like out to dinner with us to the place with the best chicken wings you'll ever have, just tell him. What's he going to do? Break up with you?*"

They both snicker at the joke, but I don't quite understand what's so funny about it.

"Enough, Wren," Virgil sighs. He puts the phone back to his ear, taking it off speaker. "I'll see if she wants to go. *I'll see.* But I'm not going to *make* her if she doesn't want to." I start to move away from the rail, wondering if he wants to argue with them in peace, but Virgil snags my shoulder and pulls me back into the circle of his arms, trapping me against the rail. "It's just you two, right? No Jed, and no Kat?" He waits, sighs, and then adds, "I'll *ask*. Bye." He hangs up without another word and buries his face in my hair.

"What's wrong with Jed and Kat?" I can't help but ask, running my fingers over the bumps in the iron rail.

"Everything," he grumps, then scoffs. "They're just a *lot*. Jed is..." he trails off, looking for the right answer. "He takes a bit to get used to. Most of my friends do, but Wren and Cass are the easiest to stomach."

"Apart from you?"

"Oh, no, I wouldn't say that," he chuckles. "And Kat is loud. She's pissed off at me, and I don't think you want to see her scream at me all night."

"Scream at *you*?" I can't really imagine someone doing that and getting away with it. Not with the way I've seen him look at people. "And you don't *mind*?"

"I *mind*," he assures me. "But they're my best friends, and I'm sure I've lost my temper with them on and off. Do you want to go? They *do* want to meet you, and they'll be on their best behavior. And I'll meet whoever you want me to meet?"

My shoulders drop a little, and I look away from him, biting my lip. "You've met my mom," I point out. "That's pretty much everyone really important to me. I mean, I'm friends with my bosses and the lifeguard at the campground. But...I don't really have *amazing friends* like that."

Virgil doesn't miss a beat. He closes his arms around me and pulls me back against his chest, nearly pulling me off balance. "That's okay," he says, not asking about it. "I'll give you a couple of my friends. You can have Wren, first of all. He loves camping probably as much as you do." Virgil makes a face. "Scratch that. He loves camping more than you or I *ever* could."

"*Oh*, so I get the camping friend? That's it?" I laugh and squirm in his grip, loving that he only tightens his hold on me absently.

"You can have the stalking friend too. Cass. But I like him, so we'll have to share custody."

"Stalking friend? Isn't that kind of like the pot calling the kettle black?" I can't help but ask.

He looks down at me, gaze flat. "*Not* like Cassian," he

assures me. "You've never seen someone *stalk* until you've seen him do it. He's so *patient*. He doesn't even do it just because he wants to kill someone. I think if he liked a girl, he'd stalk her too."

"Oh wow, what's that like?"

"*Princess*, if you keep it up, then we *won't* be meeting my friends because you'll be on your back, on my bed, and probably unable to leave there for the night." There's a note of warning in his words, but it certainly doesn't frighten me.

Though I do feel relieved that we're on the top floor of his building, and there doesn't seem to be anyone around to hear us.

He waits, eyes holding mine as if inviting me to keep going. I don't. Half because I'm not sure what else *to* say, and also because I would like to meet his friends.

"Do you want to go see them? We really don't have to. They joke about it, but if I tell them no, then they'll respect it."

"I'd actually like to," I admit. "I would say to let them know about Argus, but I guess they already know about that, huh?"

His smile turns almost *sheepish*, and he looks away. The look is so surprising that my heart nearly falls out of my chest, and I try to memorize it so that I can always remember the expression. "I've told them about you," he says finally. "A little. Maybe more than a little." He clears his throat. "Are you ready to go? Do you want to shower or anything before we leave?"

It's the least subtle change of topic I've ever heard in my life, and I answer it with a snort.

16

My hand tightens on Argus's leash, and the German Shepherd glances up at me as I follow Virgil into the casual, great-smelling restaurant. It isn't loud, thank God, but I always get a little nervous whenever I'm in such a new situation.

Maybe his friends won't like me.

Maybe the restaurant will make a big deal out of Argus.

Maybe I'll fall and slam my face on the floor, and Virgil will have to take me to the ER with a bag of frozen peas held to my face.

There are so many things that can go wrong, and I surreptitiously look behind me as if to check the door but find Virgil's eyes instead.

He reaches out and touches my arm, not smiling, but the reassurance is palpable in the touch.

"You're fine," he tells me like it's a given that I *am* fine.

Really, if he knew me, he'd know I'm *rarely* anything resembling fine, and I'm more of a hot mess waiting to fall apart at the slightest problem.

I think about telling him that. The words to do so go through my head, rearranging themselves multiple times, so it's probably a good thing that the waitress shows up, beaming, and looks us over.

"I'm not going to ask to pet him," she assures me, arms curled around a couple of menus. "I know how rude that would be. But he's adorable. And I just want you to know he is seriously the *cutest* shepherd I've ever seen."

"Oh." It's not what I was expecting, but only because I've built this up to be much worse in my own mind. "Thank you! He's definitely the cutest. And spoiled," I add, making her giggle.

My cute, spoiled dog sits down on my foot and looks up, his tongue lolling, before I reach down and stroke my thumb along the center of his nose and up towards his ears.

"Cass and Wren are already here," she tells Virgil, beckoning us to follow her before taking off down the main aisle of the restaurant.

"You guys come here a lot?" I assume, glad that the hall is wide enough for all three of us to walk together easily.

"It's the only place we really go. She actually used to date Kat," Virgil explains, gesturing to the hostess who's seating us.

"Oh. *Oh?*" I can't help but say, surprise making my brows jump upward.

He snorts. "They're still good friends. They just didn't have the same life goals. And yes, she knows."

"If we break up, are you—"

"No," Virgil says, not letting me finish the question. I look at him, stunned, and he smiles before he continues. "Because we're not breaking up. Remember? We've *absolutely* discussed this, Sloane."

I know his words are troubling. Or they should be. He's

possessive, obsessed, and *problematic* in every definition of the word.

But...I don't see it that way. I love that he's confident we aren't breaking up. I love that he makes it clear how much he wants to be in my life. Sure, I'm still somewhat terrified of what he is, and I have no idea how to process a lot of what he tells me sometimes. But I'm working on it.

And if he's so fixated and obsessed with me, why can't I be that way with him? If he can do it, so can I, right? And if he really wants to be in my life like this, why *can't* I show him the unpleasant, panicking, not-so-confident side of me that I work to hide from most people I know other than my mom?

"*Finally.*" The wry voice sounds familiar, and I look up as we round a corner into a smaller, private room with a large round table taking up half of it. While it looks like it has room for a couple of other tables and the marks on the floor to prove it, tonight it's just this one, and currently, it's inhabited by three men who appear to be around the same age as Virgil.

"Your waitress will be here soon," the hostess assures us and gives me a quick smile before skirting the wall to leave the room.

Beside me, Virgil tenses and gives a quick, pointed look at a blond, blue-eyed man that sits near the corner, turning his fork over on his napkin and gazing out the window.

"He's leaving," the one who'd already spoken says, getting to his feet and coming around the table to hug Virgil. He turns and does the same to me, surprising me into silence, and again Virgil gives a little unhappy sniff at my side. "Sorry. Should I have asked permission?" He rolls his eyes and steps back. "I'm Wren," he introduces, sticking his hand out to me.

"Oh, I'm Sloane," I reply, giving him my hand. I'm surprised at how rough his palms are with callouses like he does manual labor for a living.

Does murder count as manual labor? I can't help but wonder.

The man in the corner stands, gives the other guy still sitting a quick smile, and starts to move, only for Virgil to stop him with a hand on his arm.

"Hey," he says, in a voice that's much nicer than the one he'd spoken to his friends on the phone with. "I missed you, Jed. We'll talk before you go, all right?"

Jed. His friend that he'd thought would be too much for me. And now he's leaving *because* of me.

It doesn't sit right and makes my stomach twist. My hand tightens on Argus's leash, and I take a quick breath before saying, "Why not stay?" I speak as flippantly as I can, and both men turn to look at me. "Unless Argus bothers you?"

"Dogs don't bother me." The man's voice is surprisingly quiet, and I hear a heavy southern accent that I'm not expecting.

Virgil meets my eyes, and I hold his gaze, refusing to look away or break it. I'm not afraid of his friends. Well, maybe I am a little bit.

But I don't want his friends to have to tiptoe around me or be on edge.

"I'm Sloane," I say, moving to stand in front of him and using up my social confidence for the rest of the year as I do. I stick my hand out, trying to get him to see that *I don't want him to leave*, but it takes a moment for those baby blues to find mine.

"Jed," he says and clasps my hand with a palm that's just as calloused as the other man's. "You sure about me staying?" He looks from me to Virgil like he's asking us both.

"I literally don't mind at all. I've honestly wanted to meet his friends since I knew he *had* friends," I say it boldly, glancing up at Virgil when I do.

He snorts. "So *rude* to me when we're in public," he teases, then looks back to Jed. "Yeah, man. If she's cool with you staying, then stay."

Jed smiles almost sweetly at us and goes back to his seat in the corner.

Why am I supposed to be afraid of him, exactly? He's quiet and sweet and seems more unsure of the situation than I am. Is he really a killer?

"I'm not getting up to shake your hand," the third stranger drawls, tipping his chair back until it leans against the wall behind him. If I did that, I'd be on my ass on the floor with a concussion. "Because I'd either have to jump the table or fight Virgil for the privilege, it feels like."

Virgil *tsks* and gestures for me to sit. Only when I'm seated, with Argus between Virgil and me on one side of the table, does the man who shook my hand say,

"You can introduce yourselves," Virgil hums, studying the menu like he's never seen it before. "Appropriately." His eyes fall on Wren's and hold them, but his friend only grins.

"Wren Crystal," the man beside me introduces promptly. "I like camping, long walks on the lakeshore, and–" he breaks off with a smile. "S'mores."

"Cass Byers," the man who hadn't shook my hand said. "I'm not about to give you my dating profile like some people. Except I *don't* like camping. Or s'mores."

"Tragic," I say flatly.

"Blasphemous," agrees Wren from my left.

Jed just grins, and it's Virgil that says, "that's Jed. He *also* likes camping, but he'd prefer to be somewhere much warmer than here. He was raised in Texas."

"Oh, that's cool? Metaphorically." I expect a smile, but Jed only watches me carefully, like *I'm* the dangerous one here. "Did you live in a city in Texas, or...?"

Cass glances at him as if judging if he's going to speak, and when Jed does answer, he looks back at his menu, unbothered.

"My family owns a farm down in Williamson County," he says, sitting back in his chair and looking up at me. He really *is* good looking, though I prefer Virgil. Jed seems so much less confident. So much friendlier, sure, but I find that just means he's harder to read.

But if he's here, then he must be a killer too.

"He's an amazing cook," Wren tells me, proving once more to be the most talkative of the three.

Cass shoots him a look, and even Jed looks at him in surprise, but it's Virgil that adds, "Wren's right. You don't give yourself enough credit."

Both Cass and Jed turn their glances to *me*, and I find myself a bit taken aback and confused like I'm missing something.

But Virgil just shakes his head. "I'll explain it to her later. It's fine, you guys. You act like this is any different from when Meagan was dating Kat."

"We know it's not," Wren assures him. "And you know what you're doing. It's just..." When I turn to look at him, I find him studying my face like he's not sure what to say.

"It's just that no one ever thought *you'd* be the one to find someone that you're in love with like her," Jed supplies.

In love with?

Is that what's going on?

I turn my eyes on Virgil, who's again looking at me, waiting for my reaction.

But I'm not too sure what to do.

"What was he like when you guys were kids?" I ask, cutting off the topic before it has a chance to begin.

"The *worst*," Wren groans, running a hand through his

curly black hair. Beside him, Cass nods his head in agreement, and I take that moment to look him over as I had Jed.

Again, he's gorgeous. He's very much the boy next door, with his light brown hair and the light amount of stubble on his face. Wren, with his darkly handsome looks and wickedly gleaming eyes, is the only one that seems dangerous, but only because he looks like a flirt and acts like one too.

They're so *normal*.

"He was so weird. And we were constantly having to yank the phone out of his hands so he'd stop calling up strangers and asking about their favorite movies."

Virgil groans and lets his elbows thud to the table. "That was *years* ago," he points out.

"Well, kind of," I remind him, grinning wickedly when he turns to me. "You totally called my cabin that night to get me out of my room and *breathed* at me."

"I was coming in your window."

"You were *breathing* weird."

"I was *climbing in your window!* And you didn't exactly have any complaints."

I sniff and look back at Wren with a nod. "I have many complaints. So he called up people and asked about *movies? Why?*"

"Look, I'm going to be honest with you, Sloane. I have no fucking idea."

"I knew I should never have agreed to this," Virgil mumbles from my other side as the waitress comes in for our drink orders.

By the time everyone was done eating, I couldn't be less afraid of my boyfriend if I tried. For his part, Virgil seems a bit mortified at the stories of him being weird as a kid that Cass and Wren are more than willing to tell me, and I wonder if *their* lives are safe after tonight.

"Can we leave?" Virgil grumps, getting to his feet. "Or were there any other things you wanted to tell her, so she'll think I'm an idiot?"

"Hmmm." Wren trades a look with Cass. "No? I don't think so? I'd made a list earlier-"

"Of course you fucking did, you psycho," Virgil mutters, but Wren ignores him.

"And I think we hit everything on that list. So...I guess you can leave." he nods sagely like he's doing Virgil a favor, and my boyfriend waits for me to get up before pushing both of our chairs back in.

"Then we're *leaving,*" he says. "Goodbye."

"Wait." It's Cass that speaks and gives Virgil an unimpressed look. "Since we didn't talk about it before, we're going to say it now. Kat is pissed about what happened before you left. And she deserves to know if you're not coming back for a while."

"I'll call her," Virgil shrugs. "She's not *my* boss, Cass."

"But she has cleaned up enough of your messes," Jed points out. "She's not as mad as they say, though. I saw her before coming here."

"I'll call her *later,*" Virgil says again. "Now, can we go?"

"Just remember to call her," Wren says cheerfully, waving at me. "See you soon, Sloane? Maybe I'll pack these two up, and we'll come camping with you guys."

"Oh." The idea is actually kind of a fun one. "Yeah? You'd all actually come down to the campground?"

"I won't," Cass assures me in his less-than-amused way. "But they will."

With a few more words exchanged between us, it takes a

minute before we're back at Virgil's truck with Argus in the back seat.

I sit in mine and lean back, closing my eyes and taking a deep breath as Virgil buckles his own seatbelt.

"You okay?" he asks, hand grazing the back of mine that rests on the console between us.

"Always," I lie.

"You don't have to be. And...I'm really grateful for all of that. It means a lot to me that you made an effort to get to know my friends."

"Why did you think Jed would bother me?" I ask, my eyes still closed. "He's so *nice*."

"He's..." Virgil trails off with a sigh. "He *is* nice," my boyfriend agrees. "Under most circumstances. But he's a little bit different from the rest of us, though I suppose if anyone understands him at all, it's Wren."

"Why's that?"

"Because he was born into a family that's way worse than us."

"Meaning?"

"Meaning that the reason Jed is such a good cook is because they didn't just throw their victims into the woods or to the pigs, Sloane."

It takes a moment for that to settle in, and I half-wish I could go back a few seconds before I knew.

"Holy shit."

"Yeah."

"He's a *cannibal*?"

"He's not a cannibal *anymore*," Virgil amends. "Do you wish I'd made him leave, now?"

I think about that, rolling the question around in my mind and going back to my conversations from the night. "No, I...I don't think so."

"Good." He puts the truck into gear, and it rolls back a few feet before he rests his foot on the brake again. "Sloane?"

This time I open my eyes and turn to look at him, confused.

"They were right, you know?"

"About you being a weirdo with a phone fetish?" I ask, knowing that's not what he means at all.

He searches my face, and whatever he sees there makes him grin. "Yeah," he says finally and chuckles. "Yeah, precisely that."

17

"I just don't know, Sloane." My mother sighs heavily, the sound quickly crossing to my side of the phone and relaying all of her irritation and frustration with me. *"I'm working on getting something filed so that the police make sure he can't come back. But this is just so difficult. It might be a few days, okay? How are you holding up?"*

"I'm okay," I supply quickly, not wanting her to hurry. "Actually, Virgil, umm. Asked if I wanted to visit him in Akron. So we're here at his condo for a few days."

I think the words will comfort her. She'll feel better knowing that I'm away from Anthony and he doesn't know where I am.

But she sucks in another breath and lets it out before replying, *"Are you sure that's such a good idea?"*

"What do you mean?"

"Don't you think you're moving a little fast? You haven't known him that long, right? Don't you think the two of you might need some space?"

I gaze up at the ceiling above the sofa in Virgil's condo, blinking.

"No, Mom. I don't."

"*I do. Take some time, especially right now. I just think that you're jumping into something that you might regret later.*"

The sofa cushion under my legs dips with a new weight, and I flick my gaze lower as Virgil moves to straddle me, his hands on the arm of my sofa on either side of my face as he moves to trap me more effectively.

"I don't think so."

"*Would you consider it?*"

I meet Virgil's gaze, my free hand coming up to rest along his jaw. He turns his face into it, kissing my palm, and I grin. "No, Mom. I'm fine. I promise I know what I'm doing." I say my goodbyes and hang up, just for Virgil to tug the phone out of my hand and lay it on the table beside him before coming back to rest over me again.

"No you don't," he promises me, moving to rest his weight on my hips. "You really don't. I'm so bad for you, and even your mom sees it." He moves one hand to trace up my body, sighing out in a long breath. "Too bad though, I guess."

"I'm not *afraid* of you," I tell him, just in case he needs to hear it. "You know that, right?"

"You're *a little* afraid of me," he shoots back without hesitation. "I see it in you, once in a while. Not like you were a week ago, sure. But we'll get there."

A week ago.

Has it really been just a week?

What's *wrong* with me that I'm so comfortable, so *willing* to be here, under this man and in his condo, after only a *week*?

"You can't be in love with someone you've only known a week," I murmur, hating the words as soon as they leave my mouth.

"Oh?" He leans in and kisses my cheek, then moves down my jaw. "Says who?"

"Says...everyone, probably," I reply. "You barely know me."

"I *think* we've had this conversation before, princess."

"And maybe we should have it again." I take a breath, then ask, "Why do your friends think you're in love with me? Is it because you told them you are?"

He sits up, gazing down at me with scrutiny. "No," he says finally. "I've never told them that."

"But they said–"

"They said what they *see*, Sloane. They've been telling me for days that I must be in love with you and that they didn't think I could act like this."

"...It's been *a week*," I say again, less certain this time.

"Yeah, it has. A whole *week* that I can't stop thinking about you. I hold onto you and wonder how you'd feel if I were to tell you that anywhere I go, you're coming with me because letting you out of my sight fucking sucks. Does that seem normal to you? Does it seem normal that I'm fully willing to do whatever it takes to keep you here with me?"

"I'm not leaving," I reply breathily, not sure what else *to* say.

"I'd...let you," he says finally, though he looks like he might *vomit* as he says it. "I don't want you to think you *don't* have a choice. That's not exactly very healthy of us, is it? I'd hate it. But I would respect *your choice*, Sloane."

"It's...been a week," I say once more, my words slow and maybe a little bit unsteady. "And I think maybe *I'm* the crazy one. Yeah, I'm a little terrified of you sometimes. But it's not because of what I think you'll do to *me*. Not anymore. Isn't that fucked up, though?"

"Very," Virgil assures me, rather unhelpfully, as he leans back down and nips at my lower lip.

"But I also have never, ever felt this way about anyone before."

"Oh yeah?" The seriousness evaporates from his tone, and he moves to sit up and lifts my shirt until he can trace my stomach with his nails. "Do you *love* me, princess?"

"I don't know."

"Do you *love* this serial killer who wants to ruin you every time he sees you?"

"There's probably a time limit on the serial killer status. Have you even killed anyone in the past month–?" My words turn into a yelp as he digs his nails into my skin, causing me to arch into him.

"Careful with your words." I love the way his voice gets— all growly and rough and a little bit terrifying.

It probably shouldn't be as big of a turn on as it is.

"Or you'll drag your nails along my stomach?" I ask, writhing under him as much as I can when he does just that.

"Maybe I'll do something worse." He does it again, though, his nails leaving red marks on my pale skin. "Was that your mom?"

I sigh through my nose, my hand gripping his wrist to make him pause so I can answer with any kind of clarity. "Yeah. She thinks I should slow down with you. That we're moving incredibly fast, and maybe I'm not in the right frame of mind to make good relationship decisions." I pause, thoughtful, and add. "Can I ask about your parents?"

"You *can*," Virgil hums, moving his hand again when I let go. This time he moves his nails gently across my skin, making me shiver from the feather-light touch. "But my mom is dead, and I haven't spoken to my father in a long, *long* time." He punctuates the words by twisting around my hip bone, then skimming across to the other side of my body.

"Why?"

"Because he cheated on her, remember? With my girlfriend's mom."

"Who you...killed," I repeat, making sure I have it right.

"Yeah, that one. Dad has a good suspicion of what I did. He doesn't want to talk to me, and I don't much feel like talking to him, either."

"Are you afraid he'll tell?"

Virgil shakes his head and moves when I gesture for him to so that I can sit on the sofa, legs curled under me, and face him.

"Do you want to tell me about it?" I ask carefully, not sure how he'll take the question.

Virgil's gorgeous gaze flicks up to mine, scrutinizing my expression. "Do you *want* to hear about it?" he asks, maybe a bit perplexed.

"If you want to tell me."

Carefully Virgil reaches out to run his thumb over my lip. "I killed her," he repeats. "With a knife. I waited outside her house for *hours* that night. And before that, I'd watched her for weeks. There were the phone calls I made. Though back then, I wasn't sure *what* I wanted to do on that front exactly. So they were a little sloppy." He blinks a few times, then his eyes focus on me again. "It wasn't that neat or that interesting. She was my *first*, remember? I wasn't very good back then."

He says it like he *is* good now. And I can't repress a little shiver that creeps down my spine.

"So I stabbed her. She ran from me and nearly made it to the door, but I stabbed her until she couldn't get up. She bled out, and I...just...watched." he tilts his head to the side, reminding me of a puppy in his way. "Does it bother you?"

I don't know.

It doesn't bother me as much as it should, but I just don't know.

Still, it's not the hang-up it should be.

"Not enough to make me pack up the dogs and leave," I say finally, scooting towards him on the sofa. "So you don't have to worry about that."

"I wasn't worried," Virgil assures me, resting his chin on his hand and just *watching* me. "If I was, I wouldn't have told you."

As I stare back at him, I wish I could tell if that was comforting or disconcerting.

18

With my cheek pressed to the glass of the passenger window of Virgil's truck, I stare up at the blackening sky and let out a long breath.

Two-fourteen doesn't stand a chance. If normal storms blow off its shingles and rip up some of the woodwork around the deck, *this* world-ending tempest is going to rip it right from its hinges.

And then I'll have to go around picking up the worst of it.

The sun hasn't set yet, but the campground around us as we go down the long drive towards the House is dark and shadowed. People are still out and doing their normal activities, but when I look closer, I see that it's intermingled with packing things away into campers or vehicles and casting furtive looks at the sky.

"Guess it's the storm of the century time, huh?" I murmur, twisting my hands in my lap. "I know the weatherman said that we'd have storms, but this really looks pretty severe."

"Are you afraid of storms?"

"No." I have never been, even though thunder makes me

jump once in a while when I'm caught off guard or already feeling a little off. "Are you?"

He sighs. "Maybe once, when I was a lot younger. The others used to *drag* me out in them, telling me I'd never learn to like them if I didn't push myself."

"That seems a little harsh."

"Yeah, well, you've met Wren. You know how he is. He's this weird outdoorsy creature that chops down branches with a damned machete. In *Ohio*."

I blink, unsure if he's joking, and look over my shoulder at him. "A machete? That's a joke, right?"

Virgil grimaces. "It's messy, is what it is."

Oh.

Well then.

He turns onto the road leading to my cabin, and I can't help but surreptitiously watch for Anthony, crossing my fingers in my lap as I do. If he's still here, which I hope to God he's not, I don't know what I'm going to do.

As if sensing what I'm thinking, Virgil knocks my hands apart and laces his fingers with mine. "Stop," he says simply. "There's no way in hell he's here."

"You say that," I mumble, but I don't really have it in me to argue with him.

"Look up at the *sky*, princess." God, I love it when he calls me that. And *how* he calls me that, more than anything.

Then again, he could make any word sound sexy. Pickle. Lightbulb. Moist.

Okay, probably not *moist*. Nothing can make that sound anything other than gross.

The truck stops outside of my cabin, and I get out, looking around again for any sign of, well...anything.

Unfortunately, that comes when my eyes land on the door, and I can't help but bite my lip as I stride towards it and grab the white, folded paper off the outside of it that's been taped there.

Naturally, it's not from Pat or Sam. Why would it be when that would make things too easy?

I tried to find you, but I guess you aren't here.
I'd really like to talk to you, Sloane.
We can get to a place of forgiveness, I'm sure. I miss you and your mom.
-Anthony

Every word turns my stomach a little more, like the twisting of a screw being dug through my insides.

Argus sniffs at my hand that rests at my side, and unconsciously I reach down to rub his nose, barely paying attention even when thunder shakes the trees and makes me grit my teeth.

Then, without warning, the paper is plucked from my fingers, and Virgil looks the note over, his eyes cold and unimpressed. "A place of forgiveness?" he asks, with a disdainful sniff. "What a joke. *He* doesn't get to decide if you forgive him."

"Guess it might be better if I did," I mutter, running my hands through my hair to hide my trembling. "Then maybe he'd leave me alone." I glance up, surprised to find his hazel eyes on mine.

"Do you *want* to forgive him?" The question is so simple, and even before he's done asking it, I shake my head in disagreement.

"Fuck no, Virgil. Of course, I don't want to–" He leans down and presses his lips to mine, interrupting my diatribe against the idea of *forgiving my stepdad.*

"Then don't," he purrs, pulling away and cupping my cheek in his hand. "Don't forgive him when you have absolutely no obligation or need to do so. Don't *ever* forgive him, Sloane." his smile turns savage. "Or you could let me kill him. I'd say you could kill him with me, but I don't want there to be any chance of getting caught. It would be a lot of trouble to get my friends to murder an entire correctional facility just to get you out of prison and reinvent you under a new name."

It's...maybe the most romantic thing I've ever heard. Probably.

"You'd do that?" My lips quirk into a grin as he steps closer to me. "You'd *actually* do that?"

"Princess, I'd kill anyone for you. No questions asked. No hesitation."

Okay, maybe *that's* the most romantic thing I've ever heard.

I clear my throat and pull away slightly, trying not to swoon. "We should, umm. Get the dogs and go in. Are you staying here tonight—" I'm cut off when he grabs my arm, not letting me turn away, and pulls me towards him to wrap his arms around me and bury his face in my hair.

"Play with me," he says, and it's not quite a question or a request. "No one is out. It's almost dark." He's right. The clouds and the storm have made everything almost pitch black, and the sun has all but set by now. Rain is starting to show up on the asphalt at our feet as well, so I know for a fact that most people will be tucked inside of their campers or their vehicles.

"Play what with you?"

His answering grin is nearly a complete response. *Good enough*, anyway, that I can surmise whatever he wants to do probably isn't sweet and cuddly and romantic.

Or at least, not the kind of romantic most people would ask for. But to me? This is *definitely* the definition of the word. I love when he buries his face in my neck again, and I *adore* the growl that sounds against my skin.

Is it problematic of me that I can so easily look past what he and his friends do? That I don't mind at all that he *kills people*? Sure, by his own admission he tries to only kill those that deserve it anymore. And I appreciate the idea that he never would've *actually* killed me, probably.

And that should bother me too.

But it doesn't.

Instead I can only think of how happy I am that he followed me to my cabin and that I'm here, in the impending storm, ready to let him pin me down and do whatever he wants to me.

"Maybe put the dogs inside so they don't maul me?" Virgil suggests, letting me go at last. I nod and follow the suggestion, calling both dogs to go into the cabin. He is right, and I'd hate to see Vulcan trotting around with his severed arm because my sometimes-vicious guard dog thought that Virgil was literally hurting me.

When I close the door again, I find that Virgil is much closer than I expect, and his hand on my throat pushes me back against the door so he can lean in and kiss the side of my jaw. "Do you like to play hide and seek?" he purrs against my skin.

"Yes," I reply. Even if I hadn't before this moment, I'm pretty sure this would've changed my mind instantly. I reach up to cup his jaw in my hand, fingers stroking over day-old stubble. "How long should I give you to hide?"

His answering, rueful glare makes me snicker, and his thumb presses at the side of my neck long and hard enough that I feel light-headed.

"Maybe next time you can be the hunter, princess. But not tonight." The rain is getting heavier, and starting to drum on the roof of the porch above us. "Go find a hiding place."

"How long are you going to give yourself to find me? And

what happens when you *don't*?" I challenge, my other hand going up to wrap around his shoulder.

"Hmmm." He rocks back on his heels slightly, thinking about the question. "Thirty minutes," he says finally.

"Any rules?" My heart pounds in my chest and my breath catches in excitement.

God, I want to play this with him.

I *want* him to catch me, maybe more than my competitive streak desires to win. Either would be great, of course. Though, I'd love to see what happens if he can't find me.

And I know this campground like the back of my damn hand.

"No. Except that when I find you–"

"If you find me–"

"–*When* I find you, I get to do whatever I want with you."

There's no way he'll find me that fast.

"Deal. But if you don't find me, then what do *I* get, Virgil?"

The look in his eyes tells me that's not a possibility, but I refuse to give in to that idea. I'm good at this game and on my own home turf. I have just as good a chance of winning as he does. I think.

"Whatever you want," he murmurs finally. "However you want it."

I want a lot of things from him.

"All right," I breathe, pushing him back a few steps and moving to the edge of my porch. "How long are you giving me?"

His grin turns wicked. "I'd start hiding if I were you."

"What?"

"Because I've already started counting."

"But how long–"

"If you're just going to stand here then you might as well get on your knees."

I meet his eyes in the darkness for another second before I take off, jogging out into the rain and behind the cabin so that I can climb the hill into the woods beyond.

I know this place better than him, and I turn almost immediately so that if he is following me into the trees, he won't be able to just keep going straight.

Coming out of the trees by the bear tree, I can't help but cast a look over my shoulder, making sure that I can't see any trace of him in the rain. Past one of the playgrounds, I dart into the trees on the other side, looking for the tell-tale signs of the path Pat uses when he wants to go nature watching in his tree platform.

I find it sooner than I think, jogging along it until I reach the stairs that go up to the ten-foot high platform that bridges between two thick oak trees. It's basically a treehouse, without much of the house part, though a gazebo top will keep most of the rain off of me and a rail means that I most likely won't go plummeting to my demise. Or break an ankle, more likely.

There's no furniture up here. Pat hasn't used it since last fall, and he took his foldable chairs the last time he did, but that's more than fine for my purposes tonight. I tuck myself into the darkest corner I can, relying on the darkness, the shadows, and the trees to keep me hidden in my dark clothes.

Belatedly I put my hood up, hoping it'll cover any of my pale skin that might let Virgil know where I'm hiding, before settling back once more.

A minute passes. I count the seconds, timing them with my breathing as I look out into the pouring rain. This seems unfair to him. How would he have any chance of finding me when I'm in a part of the campground he has no knowledge of?

Another five minutes pass and I relax, just a little. He's not going to find me.

After ten minutes, I start to fidget. I'm a little bit *bored*, and the rain isn't going anywhere, it seems. There's nothing out here other than the storm and the trees, as the thunder is a nice background of rumbling, booming noise.

I don't hate it, but I kind of wish I'd thought of a better idea than coming out here in the middle of the night, in the middle of a storm. I probably could've hidden somewhere closer to my cabin, then circled back around just to be waiting for him, triumphant, on his failed return.

God, that would've been such a good idea.

I turn onto my knees, hand on the wooden rail of the platform, and look out at the black forest beyond. It's too dark to make out anything except when lightning flickers through the clearing, and I let out a sigh that's unheard over the rain.

Is the rain letting up? It feels like it, with the way the drumming on the roof above me has lightened–

My phone vibrates in my pocket, causing me to jump. I grab it before it can vibrate again, and squint my eyes to read the message on the screen.

What's your favorite scary movie?

What's my....what? I have no idea what the text means, and quickly I see that it's from Virgil.

Why are you texting me? I shoot back, firing off that message and another one after it. *Are you giving up trying to find me?*

He doesn't answer for a few moments and I sit back on my heels, confused. Does he want to end our game? It is a little cold, sure. But nothing *that* bad or unmanageable. Maybe he just got bored.

Princess, princess. I never lost you. It's not my fault you didn't try to hide faster.

My heart sinks, then races. I look up again, and when lightning flickers through the clearing I see a dark-clad shape leaning against a nearby tree.

Holy shit.

Sucking in a breath, I look down at my phone, debating on what to say, when another message comes through before I can decide.

But you still have a choice here. Do you want me to catch you here, or would you like to try for somewhere else? It's awfully cold out here, and I worry about ripping your clothes off in the rain.

I don't know how to answer. My mind blazes, races, and I look at the dark figure that's holding the phone, obviously intent on my answer with indecision and anticipation warring in my chest.

And maybe just a healthy bit of fear as well.

When I don't answer, his phone blazes brighter again, and I know the message is coming right before it does.

Fine then. If you can't make a decision, I'll make it for you. But don't blame me when you end up bent over that rail you're holding onto.

He pockets his phone and starts walking toward me.

I don't think. I don't even know why I do what I do, either. But I jump to my feet and *lunge* down the stairs, sprinting back through the woods and going back in the direction of my cabin.

Do I win if I can beat him there and lock the door?

I certainly think so.

However, I don't count on how fast he is. I'm across the street, past the bear tree, and in the woods behind my cabin when all of a sudden his arm is around my neck and he pushes me against a tree, my front pushed up against the rough bark while his arm keeps my face from the same surface.

"I wasn't expecting you to run," he growls in my ear, just loud enough to be heard over the still-steady downpour. "*Fuck*, Sloane. I never thought you running from me would be such a fucking turn on." He presses his hips against mine, and I can feel just how much he liked the chase.

But I can't deny that I liked it too.

"I deserve a little extra for that," he continues to taunt, his other hand going around to the front of my denim shorts. He unbuttons them single handedly and shoves them down, enough that he can realize I'm not wearing anything underneath. "What a little slut," he adds, though the tone of his voice is anything but disappointed. "I bet you liked it just as much as I did."

Without warning he shoves two fingers into me, making me gasp and arch back against him. "It's raining," I hiss against his jaw, unable to do much more than that. "If you think you feel—"

"I *know* what I feel," Virgil interrupts. "So don't fuck with me." He fingers me open effortlessly, as though he knows exactly what I like and how to get me to respond, even though we've only known each other a week.

"You should be grateful," Virgil goes on, the arm around my neck releasing me so that he can pull my hoodie up above my breasts. My bra gets the same treatment, and his cold hands palm my breasts roughly like he's been waiting for this.

I sure as hell have.

"Why?" I ask, trying not to let my voice climb higher.

"Because you were going to run into the mud soon. And I would've felt a little bit bad about putting you on your hands and knees in the mud. I'll feel a lot better doing it here instead. *Oh*, I know!" He whirls me around, voice amused, until I can see a large, mostly flat rock that rises from the ground at a gentle angle. "Doesn't that look just perfect?"

"It looks like a rock."

He nips my neck reprovingly and walks me towards the rock, pushing me down onto it on my hands and knees. It *is* smooth enough that my palms slide against it, and nothing digs into my knees painfully.

But I'm certainly not going to admit to being *grateful*.

I flinch when his teeth find the curve of my spine, nipping and mouthing against it as he works his way down my body. He tugs off my shorts until they hang on one ankle, and I shiver in anticipation as his hands on my ass spread me apart so he can see *everything*.

Then his fingers dig into my thighs, nails sharp, and he *bites* me hard just above my hip, causing me to shriek in surprise.

His laugh, barely audible over the rain, is the only response I get before he does it again, biting the other side of my body just as hard and long enough that he can suck a mark onto my skin.

"I hope you don't mind," he tells me, leaning over me so he can be heard. "But I realized that if I don't mark you as mine, then people might not realize how off-limits you are. In fact, I'm *sure* you don't mind."

I don't get to reply. He jerks my hoodie to the side and bites down hard on the junction of my neck and shoulder, his body caging mine and not letting me move as he takes his time in bringing a mark to my skin.

My body aches, the spots he's bitten seeming to throb in time with my heart as his teeth sink into my skin.

"I want to run my knife over this pretty, pale skin again," he tells me, and the rain is definitely dying off because it's much easier to hear his husky tone. "I love the look of it against you. And I want to run the tip between your thighs...you'll let me, right?" His fingers find my folds again and slip into me, fucking me languidly as he speaks. "It's not a question. I know you'll let me. You loved it so much last time...it's not so different from the blade on your nipples. I think you'll *like* it. Actually, you'll fucking *love* it." He thrusts another finger into me, spreading me open on all three as he fucks me deeply with them. "I won't cut you. I would never cut you. I just want to tease you. You're such a good girl, and such a horny girl for me that you'll take anything I give you without question."

His fingers in me move faster, twisting so that he can run his thumb over my clit. I jump forward in surprise, but he only chuckles and pulls me right back in place.

"Don't you run from me, princess. We're so far past you running from me anymore. It's *so adorable*, and I will always love hunting you down, but I think you need to learn when you're caught, and I'm so happy to be the one to teach you what it means to be my prey."

His fingers leave my body, and I don't hear what he does next, but when his shaft brushes my entrance, it's pretty clear. I whimper, turning my face into his just in time for him to catch my mouth in a kiss.

"Good girl," he says again, and bites down on my lower lip just as he sinks into me to the hilt.

I cry out against his mouth, unable to do anything as he teases my nipples and fucks me. It doesn't help my brain to come back online that he worries at my lip, biting and licking and *purring* his approval into my mouth.

In fact, I realize a short time later, that I'm not far from coming. I shouldn't be this ready, or this turned on. But him chasing me down to catch me and fuck me like this does something to my body and my mind that will absolutely deserve a repeat so I can revisit this feeling. He sinks into me at a perfect angle, hitting deep in my body as he holds me in place as if I really am just his prey.

Fuck, that shouldn't be as hot as it is.

"Come for me," he murmurs, nipping at the shell of my ear so that I shudder. "God, you're so fucking perfect for me. On your knees like this, right where I want you, so I can breed that pussy of yours like you deserve. Come for me so I can *breed you* and we can go back home and do it again."

I can't help but whimper, but his snicker overrides it. "Did you think this was it? That we'd go skipping back and *snuggle*, princess?" He shakes his head, and I find myself trying to hold my orgasm off, trying to balance at the edge of the metaphorical cliff he has me on.

"This is going to be all night for you. If you're good maybe I'll put you on your back instead, so you can see my face as I fill you up, my hand curled around that pretty throat."

As if to emphasize the words, the hand on my breasts comes up to curl around the base of my throat instead, thumb pressing just under my jaw and barely putting any pressure there.

"Don't try to wait me out," he continues with a real laugh. "You won't get any prize for winning that game, I can promise you. And you can't tell me any of that sounds bad, does it?"

I shake my head, biting my sore lip. It sounds *amazing*, but I'm feeling stubborn. I want to make him work for it.

Unfortunately, he's so good with how he fucks me, that it's quickly becoming a losing battle.

"I know how much you want to be my good girl, princess. I can feel how much you want to come. You can't lie to me when my cock is buried in your pussy." He gives a rougher thrust as if to illustrate the point. "Maybe you're just trying to get me to be a little rougher with you?" He doesn't lessen his pace or the force of his movements. It's a jolt every time he thrusts into me, and his angle is just right that I feel like I'm seeing stars. "I don't mind, princess. I'm not going anywhere, remember? And I certainly don't have anything to do tomorrow. If you want to make me work for it, then I'm going to make sure that I've wrung every bit of satisfaction out of you that I can." I gasp softly, fingers clenching against the rock under me. It's a small movement and an even smaller sound. I'm so close, and I hope he hasn't noticed.

Too bad for me that he notices everything.

"You're going to come." It isn't a question, but I try to laugh anyway.

"You think I am." My voice is tight. The words are a lie, and I don't know what I'm trying to prove.

"Oh we're mouthy tonight, aren't we? You're really asking for it."

"Am I?"

God, I'm close. My thighs tense, and I know I can't keep doing this for much longer. Not even the cold rain on my skin is enough for me to not think about the burning need in my body and the way he's just so perfect.

"Tell me again you aren't. Say it to me one more time."

I open my mouth to say it, and his hand on my throat tightens. His other snakes around my body, and he presses it flat to my lower stomach so that there's no chance of me going anywhere other than where he wants me to be. One of his knees is braced on the rock next to mine, and I hadn't thought he could fuck me any more thoroughly than he is.

But I was definitely wrong.

"Come on," he goads in my ear. "Tell me again. Tell me you aren't about to come, princess."

I can't. I can't say anything, because I'm holding on to this cliff with my fingernails at this point.

"Tell me, and I'll agree. We'll go back to your cabin and watch movies. I'll comb your hair and we'll cuddle."

I'm going to come.

"But if you can't tell me and you *do* come, then I'm going to take that as you *want* me to breed this pussy until morning. You *want* me inside you, making sure nothing escapes until morning. You want that, princess? Want me to keep you where you belong? Under me and full of my cum?"

I lose my grip and all but scream. The noise is ripped out of me just like my orgasm is, and I fall to my elbows under him on the rock. Only his quick movement catches me, pulling me back against him instead as his pace becomes erratic. As I come around him he lets out a groan of approval, finally slamming into me one more time and holding me there as he finds his release as well.

I barely notice. I'm too busy enjoying the aftershocks and tingles of my own orgasm to discern anything else until he pulls me to my feet and helps me pull up my shorts.

"Cabin's over there," he tells me, making sure I'm steady on my feet as he meets my eyes with a wolfish grin. "And if you're not on your bed with your ass up and waiting for me in five minutes, I'll just take you down and fuck you wherever you happen to be. Understand, princess?"

"You say that like it's a threat," I point out, unable to hide my grin.

He laughs softly and reaches out to run his thumb over my lower lip. "I'd prefer to think of it as a promise."

19

I'm right, of course.

Two-fourteen never stood a chance.

I stand at the edge of the driveway and wish that I'd stayed in bed, called in sick, and curled up with Virgil and the dogs instead of coming out here to my *job*.

God, why can't I just be someone's trophy wife? Does Virgil make enough, I wonder, for me to stay at home, lounge, and look dramatic? It's what I'm made for, obviously. Not physical, manual labor.

Until then, however, I don't really have a reason *not* to help. Especially when it's clear that we're going to need more than me, the owners, and Raven to do much more than some damage control. Especially since the people who own two-fourteen, or what's left of it, aren't even *here*.

"We're really going to do their work for them?" I grump, glad for the first time that Vulcan is still with Virgil at the cabin. Argus is with me, of course, but I don't need to worry about him getting into anything. He'll stay where I put him unless he needs to do something for me. In that case, I'd prefer he let me know instead of letting me fall face-first into a pile of nails and splintered wood.

"You'd think they'd be here," Raven agrees, her arms folded over her chest. Both of us look like we'd rather be anywhere but here, and I don't know how to fix the look on my face that promises that fact.

"Right? It's their camper. Their piece of junk that's been an eyesore on the campground for *years*." If Raven and I have one thing in common, one hobby really, it's bitching. We're good at it, and together we're unstoppable.

We're also going to have to start cleaning up. There's no way around it, and I shrug my shoulders in defeat with a groan. "Come on. We can ask for a raise later."

"We're not getting a raise," she mutters but follows me down towards what remains of the camper and the deck. The roof had just been fixed, which is a tragedy, and the whole thing looks like it was hit by a truck instead of just a pretty bad storm.

"So..." Raven works beside me, tossing rubble into a pile and making sure there's nothing dangerous on the ground for when the surveyors come to look at everything. "I saw you leave the other day with that guy staying in cabin six."

"Oh?" I ask mildly, my heart skipping a beat. "Help me with this?" One of the larger sections of the deck is still almost in one piece, though not where it needs to be, and Raven immediately grabs one end of rough, splintered wood to help me drag it closer to the other rubble.

"Yeah. Are you keeping secrets from me? I didn't think you had a boyfriend. Or is this your summer dreams hookup of your life? You know, like from *Grease*?" Her tone is light and teasing. I know her, and if I asked her to knock it off, she would.

Instead, I frown and snort at her words. Virgil is no Danny Zuko, and I'm a *far* cry from Sandy. "It's not like that," I promise her. "He's.." I suck in a breath as we drop another piece of floor. "He's my boyfriend."

"How long have you been with him?"

"Not that long."

"What's he like? Did he come down here just to see you?" She glances up at the cabins on the ridge above us, her gaze shrewd. "I notice his truck isn't up there this morning."

"You can't even *see* the vehicles at the cabins from this side," I point out, glaring at the rest of the trash we still have to pick up. "So, how do you know if he's there or not?"

"I don't need to," she replies. "I *know*."

"Stalker," I tease.

She shrugs one shoulder, looking pleased with herself. "Maybe. But seriously, I'm *dying*. I need to live vicariously through you, Sloane. Just tell me one thing." She stands straight, sucks in a breath, and looks me dead in the eye. "Is he *kinky*?"

I want to tell her no because it's not *really* any of her business, but a smile cracks over my lips, and she nearly *shrieks* with delight at my silent, embarrassed answer.

"I fucking *knew it*. He *looks* like it, and I *knew*."

"You can't tell if someone's kinky based on their looks."

"Yeah, you definitely can. Maybe you're just bad at it."

It takes the better part of the day for us to go through everything. I never see Virgil and wonder if he's spent the whole day lounging in the cabin or making campfires. It doesn't seem like him to do that, but I also haven't *seen* him.

Surely if he were around, I would've at least seen some trace of him, right?

With the storm damage and everyone cleaning up, Pat and Sam had decided to keep the House open an hour late, just in case anyone needed anything last minute. When they'd said they'd stay, I'd immediately volunteered, feeling bad when they'd spent most of *their* day cleaning up and also fighting with the people who owned some of the permanent sites down here.

"I'll stay," I had assured them, all but pushing them out the door. "I have to walk up the hill to go home, so it makes sense. And everything will be fine."

Sam had smiled, patted my arm, and looked practically *proud* of me. "Of course it will be," she'd agreed. "We have absolute faith in you."

That meant a lot, and I'd work to make sure they'd *keep* that faith in me.

Not that I had anything difficult to do. No one came in for the last hour, and after a few experimental texts to Virgil, I'd discovered that he had gone into Arkala before coming back to wait for me.

I'm done, I tell him, firing off the message quickly as I close up the register and lock the front door. With my key dangling around my wrist, I whistle for Argus and go towards the back door to leave that way, as well as lock it.

I'll be back in a few. I just need to walk back.

It takes him barely a minute to respond, and by then I'm locking the door behind me that I can only unlock from the inside. My phone vibrates in my pocket, drawing my attention as I walk past the crickets. A car drives by, going slow, and I don't bother looking up as I look for the message instead.

Want me to come get you?

A smile twitches at my lips. *No. I'm fine. It's a seven minute walk, at best.* He isn't my chauffeur, and I don't want to him to think I *expect* him to come pick me up or anything.

Pocketing my phone, I look up, and for a moment, I'm confused at what I see.

The back door leads out into a narrow, covered hallway. On one side is the entrance to the women's bathroom and the huge thing of crickets we sell to fishers. On the other is a latticework wall hung with plants and a few signs from the seventies that proclaim the campground's name in beat-up, faded letters. The small hallway leads straight out to the road, which curves up and around towards my cabin.

Only this evening, the road is obstructed by a large silver car, the side beat up like it had at one point been in a minor accident, and my ex-stepfather leans against the passenger door, a lit cigarette between his lips.

Yet another reason I don't like him and never was comfortable being in his personal space. He fucking *reeks* of nicotine, worse than anyone I've ever met.

Even now, when I'm six feet away, I feel as if I can smell it. I feel like it's wrapping around me, trapping me in place, and my hands clench at my side.

Now I wish I had Vulcan with me.

"Can we talk, please?" he asks words imploring. "I've been trying to find you for *days*, Sloane. I think–"

"I don't care what you think." My voice isn't as firm or steady as I'd like it to be, and I take a step back until my back is against the glass door. "Leave."

I'm trapped, my brain is oh so helpful to remind me. *This door only unlocks from the inside.*

At this point, I'm considering trying to break the glass.

Anthony Murphy pushes off of the car and takes three steps towards me, cutting out some of the precious space between us as Argus licks my hand and whines.

I don't need him to tell me I'm panicking. I've gone from zero to one hundred really quickly, and my heart feels like it's going to slam right out of my chest. My palms are clammy, thoughts are racing, and I know that soon I'm going to feel dizzy.

Is it hot out here? Or is it just me?

"I'm not leaving, Sloane." His voice is firm but patient as if I'm still his eleven-year-old stepdaughter that he's explaining his decision to. Like *I've* done something wrong, instead of him. "I get why you're upset, but I've waited around long enough, don't you think? This is getting *ridiculous*. It's time to sit down and talk this out."

"There's nothing to talk out." I lick my dry lips and wish I'd asked Virgil to come get me. "There's nothing to *talk about*, Anthony. You..." I suck in a breath. "You tried to kill me. You were going to. I don't know how you got out–"

"I got out because the whole thing was a misunderstanding. Things have changed. *I've* changed. I just want the chance to show you and your mom–"

"My *mom?*" Anger floods my veins, mixing with the fear already there. I'm shaking now, and it's not completely due to panic. "Don't you *ever* talk to my mom again, you asshole. She deserves way better than you. And you don't have the right–"

My brave words die in my throat as he walks forward again, close enough that he's crowding my space, and I can smell more than the ghost of remembered nicotine.

As he did when I was a kid, he fucking *reeks* of it.

"I don't know what's gotten into you. You were never this disrespectful when you were a child–"

"It's not disrespectful when it's *you*." Argus tries to get between us, doing what he was trained to do when I need personal space in a situation, and does so non-aggressively as he looks between us.

If Vulcan were here, there would be a solid chance that he'd bite. But Argus isn't like that.

Anthony scoffs and looks down at Argus with frustration. "Get your dog—"

"He's doing his *job!* He's keeping you away from me, so *move.*"

He doesn't move away. Instead, he picks up his leg and harshly kicks Argus in the chest, eliciting a surprised, pained whine from the dog that has his ears flat and him pulling away, confused.

"Don't touch him!" I lunge forward and shove Anthony as hard as I can, my hands still shaking and my brain unable to focus on anything other than getting him away from me.

But Anthony barely moves. He catches my arm, his grip *harsh*, and looks at me as if he can't believe what I'm saying.

"What is *wrong with you*? You're acting like—"

"Let *go!*" My voice is loud and high, and I fight against him with everything I have. "*Let go!*" At my yells, Argus starts to bark, trying to come between us again.

"You're acting like a child!" Anthony yells, his hand on my arm tight enough that it feels like he's grinding the bone to dust. A small, rational part of my brain notes that prison apparently didn't help his anger issues with the way he's acting.

And this is precisely why Mom had left him.

"You can't be here! You can't be around me, or Mom, or—"

"Your mother made a mistake when she sent me those papers. It's *not my fault* that she pushed me into doing what I did. I just need to talk to her, and to you, and get her to see—"

"None of us want anything to do with you!" I pull backward and, to my surprise, he lets go, causing me to stumble.

Right into the door.

My head smacks against the glass, somehow not cracking it, and I shriek as pain lances through my skull.

"Get *up*. You're being overdramatic. You're going to get in the car, and we're going to go talk to your mom. Do you understand–"

"Sloane?" The voice is unmistakably Raven's, and when I look up from my spot on the concrete, I see her round the corner, confusion evident on her features as she looks from me to Anthony.

She's not alone, either. Another woman, one who looks enough like her for them to be related, is with her and looking at Anthony with just as much confusion while Argus continues to bark, the fur on his neck standing up.

"Who are you?" Raven demands, rounding on Anthony. "Liza, call the cops."

"No, that's..." Anthony puts his hands up in surrender as Liza pulls out her phone, ready to dial. "I'm leaving, all right? This got out of hand. It's *fine.*" His eyes on mine tell me that it's not fine and that he's not done.

"Get lost," I whisper, drawing my knees up to my chest. "And don't come back."

"We're going to *talk*," he reiterates. "Once you have a chance to understand–"

"She told you to leave." Raven's voice is firm. Dangerous, even, as she plants herself between him and me. He towers over her and outweighs her by half, at least. But she stares him down like she's not afraid of anything he has to offer.

I wish I could do that.

Anthony puts his hands up again and gets back in his car, driving off just as a familiar black truck rounds the corner.

"Now what?" Raven mutters, coming to help me to my feet as Virgil slams to a stop.

"It's my boyfriend," I mumble, squeezing my eyes shut against the pain in my head and the tears. Vulcan jumps out of the truck, vaulting over to inspect me and then sniffing at Argus.

Moments later, Virgil is there, cupping my face in his hands and looking at me with confusion and something else.

Something like a *threat*.

"What happened?" he demands, his voice soft and seemingly calm. But he doesn't *look* calm. Not his eyes, anyway.

God, I just don't want to cry.

"Can you-can one of you look at Argus?" I ask, my voice trembling along with the rest of me. I feel dizzy, faint, and like I'm going to vomit. "He got kicked, he–I think he's all right, but–"

"My mom is a vet. Let me look?" Liza offers, going over to kneel in front of my service dog. She feels along his chest and legs, murmuring praise to him while Virgil just meets my eyes, face close to mine.

Finally, Liza pulls back with a sigh and rubs under Argus's chin. "He's fine," she assures me. "Not even bruised."

"Wonderful," I whisper. "Awesome." I turn my gaze back to Virgil's and grip his wrists. "Can we go home? Please?"

Beside me, Raven frowns. "Do you want us to call the cops? And you hit your head pretty hard, didn't you? Maybe going back isn't the best idea."

"No, I'm fine. I'm *fine*," I promise her, in a voice that's definitely not fine. "I just want to go home. It was...he used to be married to my mom. He's gone now, though." But not for long, and the look in Virgil's eyes shows me that he knows I'm lying for the girls' benefit. "I just want to go." I offer them both a shaky smile and after a few moments, Raven nods.

"If you really want," she says finally. "Just call me if you need anything?" She hugs me awkwardly since Virgil won't let go, and her friend gives me her own sympathetic grin that just makes me want to sob.

Once they're gone, I look back to Virgil, take a breath, and say, "I really might throw up. Or faint. Or both? Maybe both. Sorry if it's both."

20

I don't move from my spot on the sofa when three knocks sound on the door. They're light, undemanding even. I frown and look up, my hand curling more firmly into Argus's ruff as he pants on the sofa beside me.

God, if I open the door and it's Anthony, I'm never going to get over it. Already I feel weird about not calling Mom, as Virgil had asked me not to. But Mom needs to *know,* especially if my stepdad is paying her a visit soon too.

I don't want him anywhere near my mom. Or me, for that matter. But Mom doesn't deserve that.

"It's just us," the muffled, familiar voice calls from the other side of the door. "Just your friendly, neighborhood campers."

Is that *Wren*? By us, does he mean Virgil, who I haven't seen much today, or Cass?

Well, I suppose there's only one way to truly find out. I get to my feet and walk to the door, opening it as Vulcan gives a half-assed bark from the bedroom.

He runs out, collar jingling and tail wagging, to inspect

Wren and Cass thoroughly while Argus just watches from the couch.

"Hello," Wren greets, looking at me for permission as his hand hovers over Vulcan's ears. I nod, and he kneels down, proceeding to instantly go into baby talk mode as Cass just watches him from a few feet behind.

"I did not know you were such a dog person," I remark, leaning against the door frame and letting out a long breath of air. "Really, it's....cute?" That doesn't seem like the right word, exactly, but I'm going to go with it.

God, I'm so tired.

"How are you?" Cass moves straight to the point, drawing my gaze up to his, and I stare at him for a few seconds before shrugging off the question.

"I'm okay. I'll *live* anyway. What are you guys doing here?" They don't make me uncomfortable or scare me. They just seem...*normal*. For the most part. Except, obviously, for a few key differences between them and most people that are negligible at best. Probably.

"I'm fine, I guess. I'm just trying to figure out why Virgil doesn't want me calling Mom!" I raise my voice, expecting him to saunter out from behind the deck or a tree.

Instead, Wren straightens, and both of them look at me like I may have slightly lost it.

"He's not here," Cass says quietly, putting me out of my misery.

"Oh. *Oh?*" My eyebrows jump upward. "Where is he?"

"He is stalking your stepdad, making a note of where he's staying and figuring out a good place to dump the body. I *think* he's decided dismemberment will work best here, but I'm not sure yet. Cass?" Wren turns to look at his friend, black curls falling to frame his face.

Cass shrugs. "I thought we were still on the burning plan. That's why he wanted us to get the trashcan, remember–"

"Sorry, *what*?" I can't help but interrupt, and my voice is higher than I intend it to be. "What did you just...are you talking about *murder*?"

"Can we come in and talk about this?" Cass asks from behind his friend. "I don't like being in the open as much as these two when we discuss things."

"What? Oh umm. Sure?" I back up, calling Vulcan in as well, and the two of them walk inside and look around my small cabin.

"I would have *loved* to live somewhere like this when I was younger," Wren says, going to the kitchen and pulling out one of the chairs at my tiny table. "Too bad it's not closer to the lake."

"Your mom owns a campground, right?" I ask, going back to the sofa and sitting next to Argus. "That's what Virgil said?"

"She *does*. And she was always really strict with me as a kid."

"Well, you did almost drown," Cass points out and sits in the chair opposite him.

"Hey, *hey*." Wren points a finger at his friend. "I'd rather almost *drown* than have to hear the jokes about stabbing my sister in the chest for the rest of my life, man."

I'm learning to let those comments go. I let them wash over me like a wave and just...don't think about them.

It's the only way I can really get through this sane, I've decided.

"So, back up. But like really back up. I don't want to hear about people you've killed," I assure him. "You're here...*why*, again?"

"To...kill your stepdad?" They look at each other as Wren speaks. "Were you not going to help?"

"I didn't even *know*."

"Virgil said he thought you knew. Or at least that he was planning this," Cass points out.

I open my mouth to reply, but the door opens again, heralding the return of my boyfriend. He looks between us, and at my slight scowl, before holding his hands up in surrender.

"I can explain?" he offers, a lopsided smile going to his lips. "I can probably explain, princess."

"*Oh*." Wren draws out the word. "So you *didn't* tell her. Nice."

"I thought we'd *ask* her. And if she says no, then you guys are going home without any trophies." He looks between them, eyes steely, before turning to me. "So, we would like to kill your stepdad," he says, sitting down in the scant room between Argus and me. Offended, the dog huffs and hops off the sofa, following Vulcan into the bedroom as I watch.

"That's umm….huh." I don't know what else to say. Obviously, I *should* say no. The same way I *should've* said no to Virgil staying in my room that first night.

But here I am.

And Anthony is still around here somewhere, looking for another chance to hurt me or going to 'talk' to my mom.

"Can we talk about it?" I ask, feeling a little bit flighty like there's a bird trapped in my chest. "I just…it's kind of a big deal. I'd really like to talk about it."

"What's to talk about? We find him, we kill him, we clean up," Wren shrugs. "We can make it terrifying for him if you want him to suffer. Or we can make it quick." It's so strange that he talks about it like it's just business. Just a *job* to do that he's done a thousand times before. Well, maybe it is.

"Death just seems so final." But even as I say it, I know that I wouldn't mind him being dead. Ever since he showed up the first time, I've fantasized about letting Virgil do what he's threatened.

And right here is my best shot.

I turn to face my boyfriend, my knee brushing his thigh. He splays his fingers on my leg, gazing at me, and I watch him with the same silence, the same scrutiny.

"What if you guys get caught?" I ask finally, voicing my deepest fear about the whole thing. "I don't want you going to prison. Especially because of me. And what if my stepdad has a weapon? He could *kill* you."

"*Princess.*" he purrs the nickname, and distantly I hear Wren choke on his spit. Virgil leans forward, his hand tightening on my thigh, and runs his hand over the bruises from my stepdad's fingers that had formed the night before. I flinch, the area sensitive, and he lightly covers them with his own hand as if he can will them away just like that. "We're not going to get caught. We're not going to get killed, either. If something did happen. Say, Wren fucks up and gets blood everywhere, maybe."

Cass snorts into his hand, prompting me to glance his way, but Virgil pulls me back with a guiding hand on my cheek so that I'm looking at him again.

"Things have happened before. Usually because of him." He flicks his gaze towards a very affronted Wren. "And we've almost been caught. But we've been doing this for a very, very long time. And we have *very* good friends. We're not going to jail. We're not going to die. Not now, not ever, and certainly not for your disgusting *stain* of a stepfather. I promise."

He says it so firmly and with so much assurance that it's impossible not to believe him. It's absolutely not even a possibility in my mind that he's wrong when he's looking at me like this.

I reach up and encircle his wrist with my fingers. "How are

you going to do it?" I ask, the words falling from my lips like stones.

I shouldn't want him to.

I shouldn't say yes.

But I don't want him near my mom and me again for another chance at us. Hasn't he proved he's dangerous? Hasn't he proved that he hasn't changed one *bit* from how he was when I was a child?

He has, and I'd be stupid to believe in anything else. He's shown me who he is, what he is, and what he wants. I don't need to be hit in the head with another door to get that he's not a good person, and this won't be a good situation for Mom or me in the long run.

Besides, he had his chance. He went to *prison*, for fuck's sake. If he was going to change, he would've done it and gone far from here when he got out. Not come straight to my home and tried to convince me to 'forgive' him by using intimidation and violence.

He's the same piece of shit he always has been, and the realization makes something just *click* inside my chest.

I *want* Virgil and his friends to kill my stepfather. I *want* to see him dead on the floor, bleeding out, and burning in a barrel after the deed is done.

Well, okay, I don't really need to see him burned to ash. That probably doesn't smell so great, and I might vomit.

"I'm going to cut him up. I'm going to bleed him for you so that you can see how red his blood is." He draws closer until his forehead is pressed against mine. "Wren has his machete. It's messy and a pain to clean up, but I'll let him chop him up for you. So *you* can watch him scream with that big blade sawing him in half."

I shudder, wondering how I'm ever going to come back from how sexy he's making this sound. His hand settles on my throat, but when I try to glance at the others, Virgil keeps me in place, face directed at his.

"And if you want, you can watch. I'll have him beg for whatever you want. I'll have him scream and cry out that you're the only mercy in the room he could ever have. But we both know you're not. You want to see him bleed more than any of us. You *deserve* it, you know."

"I do?"

"You absolutely do," Wren remarks, drawing a quick glance from Virgil.

"Just tell me that we can. Tell me we can kill him, Sloane." Virgil's lips brush mine, and it's so unfair that he's using every tool in his arsenal against me right now to get me to agree to *murder*.

But in reality, though I'll never admit it, I doubt it would've taken any of this.

"Okay," I whisper and kiss him hard, not minding that the other two are *right there* and definitely watching.

Virgil pulls away first, thumb on my lower lip. "You're telling me yes?" he clarifies. "You'll let me kill him for you?"

"I *want* you to kill him," I agree. "Because the world doesn't need a leech like him."

21

If my heart beats any harder, I worry that it'll escape my chest entirely.

Whether he just knows or it's obvious, Virgil reaches over to cover my hand as we sit in the truck, an easy smile on his features. "It's going to be fine," he promises. "For us. Not your stepfather."

"Wonderful," I murmur and hope I'm not about to puke. I don't *love* him. Nor do I feel bad about Anthony's impending demise.

He deserves it. He wasn't a good guy before my mom, a detail we'd learned after he went to jail, and he isn't a good person now.

I suck in another breath, gulping air into my lungs like water. Hell, the oxygen even *feels* like water, with how heavy it sits in my lungs.

"Do you want us to go?" It's dark outside, and I can barely see Cass's profile as he leans forward to speak quietly. "We could take care of things. That way you can stay with her."

Virgil holds my gaze, thinking.

"It's okay," I say, aware of how excited he's been to do this. I know he wants a piece of Anthony, and I'm sure he'd enjoy hunting him down to get it. "You can go—"

"Let's do that," Virgil agrees, unbuckling his seat belt and mine. "Why don't you two go in and secure everything, and we'll go in when you're done?"

Wren and Cass open their doors, the indoor lights of the truck staying off, and in the mirror, I can see the flash of the large machete Wren has as he takes it off the seat.

"It's really okay," I murmur, repeating my words. "I know you want to—"

"I want you," he argues. "I want to sit here with you and wait until they're done." The truck doors close quietly, the lights going out again. "I promise, Sloane. There's nowhere I'd rather be than right here."

"But I thought you wanted to...you know. Go be *you* and grab him or something?" I know he does or did, at least.

But Virgil just shakes his head and leans forward to brush his lips to mine. "It's *fine*," he says. "You're more important than anyone I want to kill."

"How romantic?" I'm not sure if it *is* romantic, but I'm going to pretend it is all the same.

"It's the most romantic I've ever been. *Relax*, princess." He pushes me gently back against the seat, his fingers tickling over the back of my hand. "We just need to wait. Just for a little while."

"How little of a while?"

In the dim glow of a far away street lamp, I can just barely see him smile as he leans back against his own seat, his hand never leaving mine. He draws figure eights on my skin, then switches to inscrutable patterns as his deep breaths move slow and even throughout the otherwise silent truck.

It can't be more than ten minutes, maybe fifteen, when his

phone vibrates in the console. He moves easily, lazily almost, and brings it up to his face to read the screen like he has all the time in the world.

"Do you want to come?" he asks, putting the phone in the jacket of his hoodie.

My lips form the word no. I don't want to go. I want to stay right here and wait for his triumphant return.

But instead, I take a deep breath and say, for some crazy reason, "Yeah. I...I do. Can I?"

"Of course, you can." He gets out, and I do the same, moving quickly to stand beside him as he closes the door and locks it. Still just as quickly, I follow directly behind him, like I'm attached to his shadow and trying to melt into it.

For Virgil's part, he never once slows. He never looks anything but confident and appears to belong here with absolute certainty.

This is crazy, is all I can think of. It's *crazy* because it's not like we've done a full vetting investigation. We haven't gathered reasons or evidence. We don't have *real cause*.

But here I am, following my boyfriend in to kill my stepdad.

I must be fucking insane.

The front door of the small, rundown house opens, and we just stroll on through like we're meant to be there. Like Anthony Murphy has invited us inside. My steps slow, and I look around, realizing that this must be a place he's renting. There's no way he's bought all this furniture in such a short amount of time. No way that he decorated this place, either.

We turn the corner, and my heart nearly drops when I see my stepfather tied to a chair in the middle of a room, the furniture shoved to the sides.

Both Cass and Wren lean against opposite walls, their faces

obscured by shadow as my stepfather looks up at the sound of my footsteps.

"*Sloane?*" he gasps, the words slurred a little through swollen lips and what might be a broken nose. "Sloane, is that you? Get me out of here. Tell them to *stop!*"

"No," I whisper, without really meaning to. I move further into the room, gazing down at him as my stomach twists itself into what's probably an origami swan. It feels that intricate, anyway. I feel like my insides might betray me, and I might really get sick, even though I haven't yet.

But I don't feel *bad* for him. I feel nervous about the situation.

"I asked you to leave me alone," I say quietly, choosing my words with care. "I asked you so many times. But you want to go threaten *Mom* too?" I shake my head. "You never should've come to find me, Anthony. You should've gotten out of prison and just left us alone."

"You needed to see that it was all a mistake. I need to convince you so I can convince your mom...Sloane, the two of you were the best things that ever happened to me."

"Well, you were the worst thing that ever happened to us."

The silence rings between us as Virgil prowls around him, standing at his back as he draws a wickedly sharp knife from the holster at his back. His eyes are on mine as Anthony tries to look at him, and there's a question there that I don't know how to answer.

"Fine," Anthony whispers, licking his lips nervously. He jerks at the bonds securing him to the chair and tries to wriggle free with no success. "I'll leave. I won't come back, all right? You've made your point."

"Liar." I'm surprised at the vehement frustration in the word. Surprised because I *mean it*, and I know he *doesn't*. "You'll always come back. You're like a pathetic, miserable cockroach. You just won't leave us alone." I clench my hands into fists at my sides to hide their shaking. "I want you to leave, but it doesn't seem to be happening the easy way."

Taking a deep shuddering breath, I add. "I just want to know something. Please. Tell me the truth, and..." I know he has every reason to lie to save his own skin. I need to make the truth appetizing. I need to make it worthwhile.

"Tell me the truth, and I won't let them kill you."

"Do you promise?" he asks, and I nearly smirk at the similarity to what I'd asked Virgil so many times before.

I shrug, trying to look like I agree with him. "Yeah, Anthony. I don't want you to die. I'm not a killer. I *swear* that if you tell me the truth about what I'm going to ask, I'll make them let you go."

None of the men do more than look up at me with interest.

They know I'm lying. It's obvious to them. Probably just as obvious as it is to me. There's no way anyone in this room could believe it since we're this far unless they have nothing else to grasp onto.

Like Anthony.

"Fine. Ask your question. I promise I'll tell you the truth."

"Why did you take me out of school that day?"

I'm sure that I know. After all these years, I've come to my own conclusion, sure. But I want to hear it from *him*.

Anthony takes a deep breath and looks between Wren and Cass warily. Both of them hold blades, though Cass's is much smaller than the literal machete in Wren's hand. Then he turns to look at me again, hair flopping over the baldness of his crown.

"Because I knew it would hurt your mom," he mumbles. "I *knew* it would hurt her, and I thought it would mean she'd have to tear up those divorce papers. I couldn't think straight. I was drunk, which you know, and everything was spinning. I thought that if I could just get you away from her *lies* and her *poison*, that you could see my side of things and talk her round."

His side of things? Like he hadn't spent weeks tearing her and me down verbally and somewhat physically before Mom had the strength to say *enough*?

What side of things was his, exactly? I'd lived it just as clearly as he had, and I definitely didn't need to be told that I was wrong. Not then, and not now.

"Why did you decide to kill me?" My voice trembles as I say it. I don't want to ask, but I need the answer. I *need* to know that I was right all those years ago.

He looks at the two men again. "*Swear* if I tell you that you won't let them kill me," he whines again, his voice high and frightful.

I offer him the fakest, most reassuring smile I can muster. "I *promise*. They won't do it. They just wanted to help me scare you. Just tell me the truth and—"

"To get back at your *mother*," he spits, the words like acid in his mouth. "I didn't care about *you*. Not when I decided that. Sorry, Sloane, but it's the truth. I wanted to get back at her, and the only way I knew how was through you. I was *drunk*." He uses it as an excuse when it only serves to fuel my anger. "But you were just some kid from an affair she had. I could've given her a real family."

My blood runs cold. I've never hated someone as much as I do right now, and behind him, Virgil shifts with a sigh. "Are you done?" he asks, eyes locked on mine. "You don't need to hear his bile. He's nothing, Sloane."

He's nothing.

He really is *nothing*.

"Yeah," I state, forcing my voice steady as my nails dig into my palms. "I'm done. You can do whatever you want."

Anthony's eyes go wide, his face falling open in fear. "You said—"

"I lied," I say coldly. "It's something I'm getting better at, actually. I fucking *lied*, and what are you going to do about it?" My mouth twists into a grin as Virgil stands at Anthony's back, the knife coming to rest against his throat as he tangles one latex-gloved hand in Anthony's hair. "Sue me?"

Anthony doesn't get the chance to answer.

My stepfather only gets the chance to gasp, his mouth going wide in an 'o' shape as Virgil runs the blade cleanly along his throat, pulling his head back so that blood sprays upward and lands a few feet from my shoes.

I thought I'd be sick. I thought the sight of him gasping for air through a ruined throat would send me to my knees or have tears in my eyes. I thought I would *care,* at the very least.

But I don't.

I don't care one damn bit, and I find that my eyes are glued to the spectacle in front of me, like a disaster I can't look away from.

Finally, when his gasps are done, and Wren hefts his body over one shoulder, Virgil sheathes the blade and walks forward to push stray hair from my face affectionately.

"Good girl," he murmurs, hand on my cheek. "I always knew you had it in you."

22

The door closes behind me, and I stare up at the mini chandelier of the foyer, a word I never thought I'd have a use for.

"Wow," I say, only half paying attention to Vulcan, who's moved to the end of his leash to greet Virgil as he comes out of the kitchen. "How much did you pay for this? And also, being a reporter pays *this* well?"

The house isn't a mansion by any means. And I doubt real estate prices in Arkala are as cringe-worthy as somewhere like Akron or Cincinnati. But still. The house has to be three bedrooms, at least, and probably at least twenty-five hundred square feet.

It's a house for a *family*, not one person.

Even if that person is Virgil.

"Being a reporter pays…somewhat well," Virgil admits, letting Vulcan off his leash. "Can I let Argus go?" he asks, hand hovering over the leash clip as I turn to look at the room around me.

"Yeah, sure. So long as you don't mind them making a

mess." I doubt they're going to do that. They don't *make* a mess, and neither of them is dirty. But they are dogs, and this is a new house.

"I'm sure we'll make more of a mess than they *ever* will," Virgil chuckles, unclipping Argus. I give him his release word, and the dog trots off to follow his friend, now that he doesn't have to worry about me for a few minutes.

"Getting tired of my cabin?" I snort. "Are you planning on hosting sleepovers here on the weekends?"

"Well, yeah." He beckons me with a crook of his fingers, and I follow him through the house easily enough. It's impressive. Like I'd thought before, not a mansion. But still a nice, one-story house with an open floor plan and three bedrooms. It's furnished, so I wonder if he bought it that way, and when he opens the fridge, he gestures to it like it's something of note.

"This is *real food*," he tells me, pretending like he's putting on a show. "Not frozen. *Real*, raw food."

"I didn't think you could cook," I say, sliding onto one of the barstools. "And I'm more interested in your bedroom than your fridge."

"Be interested in *all of it*." He closes the fridge and goes to the pantry, repeating the process like an overdramatic thespian.

"I get it. You don't like my frozen food consumption. *I get it*," I tease as he beckons me again and leads me down the hallway, past a sunken dining room where dog bowls are set up along one wall and already filled with water.

It's surprisingly thoughtful, and my steps slow as I look at the dining room properly, another mini chandelier catching my attention.

"You coming?" he hums, coming back to catch my hand in his. "Because we aren't in the bedroom yet."

From somewhere else in the house, Vulcan barks, and I wonder if he and Argus have found something to wrestle over.

Well, I did warn Virgil. If something gets broken or they eat one of his shirts, then that's on him.

"Okay, *okay*," I follow him, not having any other choice with his hand around my wrist until he pushes open the door into the large, primary suite of the house.

The bed inside, and the attached closet with rows and rows of storage, are impressive. So is the bathroom that connects to the far wall that houses a shower and jacuzzi.

"You *must've* paid a fortune for this. Are you broke now? Is this you telling me that you're going to get a job as a sex worker?" It's a joke, and he scoffs at the words.

"Yeah, princess. That's absolutely what I'm telling you." Before I can reply, he pulls me closer, only to push me down onto the large bed and crawl onto the mattress behind me. I roll onto my back once my head finds the pillows and manage to kick my shoes off so I don't get them on his nice, clean sheets.

Virgil, who is still wearing his shoes like a heathen, crawls over me until he's right above me, arms and thighs caging me in as he stares down at me with intensity.

My smile fades slightly as I watch him, my hands on the pillows above me. "What?" I murmur finally. "What's wrong?"

"Nothing," he breathes, leaning down to kiss me. "You know how much I like you under me. In this case..." he looks around, then shrugs one shoulder. "I've been wanting to get you here for days, princess. Right into my house, in my bed where you belong."

"I still can't believe you *bought a house* in Arkala."

"I was offered a job here," he replies instantly, like he's prepared the answer long before I got here. "Akron is a little problematic for me right now. So I need a place to wait things out for longer than my ten-day cabin stay." He reaches up and cups my jaw, running his thumb over my lip. "Why don't you stay here with me?"

"For tonight?" I nip at his thumb, my heart pounding in my chest. I have a feeling he doesn't mean for *just* tonight.

I have a feeling he means for much, much longer than that.

"Tonight. Tomorrow. For as long as you want. It's big enough, even if you wanted your own room. Hell, you could have *two* rooms. And it's only a few miles from your work."

My heart flutters like a little bird in my chest, and my lips part as I stare up at him, suddenly just as nervous as I had been the first time he'd broken in.

"You're asking me to move in with you," I state, though none of my words have the tone of a question.

"Yes," he agrees without hesitation. He, too, looks a little unsure. Like he can't tell what I'm going to say, for all he's told me I'm easy to read.

But maybe I'm not as easy to read as he'd thought.

"I've known you for *two weeks*," I remind him, looping my arms around his neck. "Two *weeks*, Virgil. And you want me to move in with you? Doesn't that sound crazy to you?"

"A lot of things that should sound crazy to me normally don't." He turns to kiss my arm, lips warm against my skin. "This is definitely one of them."

I'm not sure. The realization rings through my brain. It's not that I don't *want* to. I'm just nervous. I'm afraid.

I don't know what that would mean for me if I did move in here with him.

"I'm..." I don't want to disappoint him. My fluttering heart turns to lead, but before it can go much further, Virgil presses his thumb harder against my lip, and a soft smile curls his lips.

"Not right now. I don't want to *force* you, princess. I'll always be here. And if that means that you're just here for sleepovers and living at the cabin still?" he shrugs one shoulder. "I don't mind."

"You really don't?"

"Not at all. You were *made* for me, Sloane. And maybe that seems a little crazy for me to say since we've only known each other for fourteen days." He moves to lay down over me, hovering just above my body as his front brushes mine. Instinctively I bring my thighs up around his hips, and he cradles my face in his hands.

"Sleepovers," I say finally, grinning up at him. "I'm here for the sleepovers, at *least*. But I'm not learning to cook just because you don't like my frozen food."

"So we'll let Jed move in?" Virgil offers, kissing me sweetly. "I'm telling you, he's an amazing cook."

"*Sleepovers*," I repeat because I don't want him to get the wrong idea that he can bribe me into moving in with him even with the promise of good food.

EPILOGUE

"Wake up, princess. We're not fucking *done yet*." His fingers plunge deeper into me and I open my eyes, only half aware I'd closed them.

"How long does it take before it's no longer a *sleepover* and you just live here?" Virgil's voice sounds like a low purr as he continues, and while the question *seems* like a legitimate one, I know it's not.

It can't be since there's a gag holding my lips open, and my teeth are sunk into it like a chew toy.

I moan when his fingers delve deeper into me, and the knife that had been tossed aside a few minutes ago suddenly trails across the skin of my inner thighs once more. My arms twist in the soft cuffs that keep me in place.

I can't move, even if I want to.

"Because I have to tell you." The tip of the knife digs into my sensitive skin just enough for it to be almost painful. Then it's gone again, and his mouth is there instead, nipping and biting over my thigh. "You've been here for a while now, and it doesn't seem like you're leaving anytime soon."

I *want* to remind him that he's kept me here for the better part of the day, cuffed to his bed as he takes his fill of whatever he wants from me.

So far, that's resulted in three rounds of him fucking me much too slowly and much too teasingly.

I hate it.

Except, I don't.

I shudder as his fingers are replaced with his shaft, and he sinks into me with a groan and leans on his arms so we're nearly face to face.

My knees lift, one leg curling around his as I sigh and stare at him over the gag, my eyes wide.

"You always feel so good for me, princess," he purrs, one hand going to my hip as our bodies meet. "Like you really were made for me. You're fucking *perfect*. My perfect, sweet little slutty princess."

Another shudder goes through me at his words, and my eyes close as he starts to move once more. This time I can't help but whimper. I'm still so sensitive from everything else we've done today, and it's a combination of *too much* and *so fucking good*.

"Am I being mean to you?" he asks, his movements speeding up like the idea is an appealing one. "Am I being too *rough* with my princess?" I love when he calls me that. Why wouldn't I? *How* can I not, when his voice is just such a turn on?"

But I nod anyway, opening my eyes to make sure he knows I'm answering him.

A slow smirk crawls over his lips, and he sits up enough that he can put one hand gently on my throat, being careful not to push down. "Well, that's too bad, isn't it? I can't help how sexy you look under me like this. Though I can't decide..." His movements pick up, and I whine as I try to move to relieve some of the overwhelming sensations. "Whether I like you more like this or more on your knees. What do you think?"

My answer is a long, high moan as my back arches off the bed.

It's so hard not to come when he's had me on edge *again* for the past few minutes.

"I know, *I know*," he coos sweetly, moving his hand to cup my cheek instead. "I'm really just the worst. Only, I don't think you mind so much. Are you going to come for me? Hmm? Are you going to come while I fuck your pussy for the fourth time for me? You were *made for this*, weren't you? Made for me to play with. I must've done something really good in a past life to get rewarded with you, huh?" His chuckle is grating, and I know he's just as close as I am.

It's too bad I can't reply, but after the fourth smart-ass remark of the day to see how far I could push him, he'd decided it was time to break out the new ball gag. It's hotter than I'd expected, even if my jaw is aching.

When he shifts for a better angle and his thrusts become harder, I shudder and let my hips arch to meet his. My eyes close hard, and one of his hands finds my bound one.

"Come for me, princess," he murmurs, mouth close to my ear. "You know how much I love to feel you come around my cock." A nip to my ear and his fingers curling with mine is all it takes. I gasp around the gag as I come, my back arching as sharply as it can with me being tied down and him over me. My orgasm is weaker than my first and second but just as sharp and pushes me a little further towards what is probably insanity at having come so many times in such a short period of time.

Virgil buries his face in my throat and growls, following me and emptying himself inside of me. It's apparently a kink of his

I hadn't known existed to push my knees apart and finger me while I'm still full of his cum and practically dripping.

Especially now that he's fucked me for the fourth time.

This time, before sitting back, Virgil reaches up and gingerly undoes the gag from my mouth before tugging it away and tossing it to the bedside table. I breathe through my mouth, sucking in deep lungfuls of air, and I'm surprised to realize that tears run down my cheeks from overstimulation.

When had that happened?

His fingers unbuckle the cuffs deftly, and he massages my wrists before letting my arms fall again.

"You're okay?" he assures, leaning down to kiss me sweetly, a move that belies his earlier intensity and words.

"I'm okay," I reply, shakily reaching up to pull him to me. He kisses me again as if he's trying to devour my mouth and possibly suck my soul out while he's at it. "By the way," I add, now that I can speak. "I'm only here *six* days a week. It's not living with you until it's all seven."

It's only six because of my transitioning work schedule. In opposition to my prior words from a month ago about *sleepovers only*, I've been here a *lot*.

Because I just can't stay away from him, no matter how much I try to tell myself to take things slow. At this point, I'm pretty past listening to my mother's voice inside my head. Especially since my mom herself has decided he's not so bad after all.

"I'll gag you again," Virgil threatens teasingly, hand going between us so that he can press two fingers into me.

I whimper, my fingers finding his hair. "I need a break," I say, half-laughing. "You have *got* to let me take a *nap*, at least."

"I'll consider it."

"It feels like you're trying to make it so I'm too *tired* to leave tonight." That had been my plan, but when his lips curl into a wicked smirk, I realize that had been *his* plan all along. "You asshole," I say without heat and slap his shoulder reprovingly. "You can't just *fuck* me into being so tired I stay the night *again*."

"Why can't I? It seems to be working very, very well." He kisses me once more like he can't get enough.

And maybe I can't either.

"I have enough toys here, and myself of course, to keep you occupied for a month. You won't *want* to leave my bed," he assures me when he pulls away.

"You're such a *jerk*." I curl my arm around his shoulders, and he rolls onto his side, pulling me onto mine.

"I'm *your* jerk," he points out, cupping my jaw and brushing his nose against mine. "All yours, and never anyone else's."

I watch him, knowing he won't ask anything of me I'm not willing to give him, and finally lean in so my lips brush his ear before I whisper, just loud enough for him to hear, "I think I might love you."

"I know you do," he chuckles, sliding his hands around my hip and shoulder so he can keep me pressed to him. "I'm just waiting for you to realize it."

"Maybe I'll hold out then, just to make you wait longer."

"Oh, *princess*." He bites my shoulder teasingly. "I'll wait as long as you need me to. You should've told me to leave, and now that you didn't, there's no getting rid of me." It shouldn't be romantic, but it is. It shouldn't make me smile and hug him tighter.

But it does.

ABOUT THE AUTHOR

AJ merlin is an author, crazy bird lady, and rampant horror movie enthusiast. Born and raised in the Midwest United States, AJ is lucky to be right in the middle of people who support her and a menagerie of animals to keep her somewhat sane. When she isn't writing, she's probably watching something scary, witchy, or being swarmed by her pigeons.

Connect with her on Facebook or Instagram to see updates, giveaways, and be bombarded with dog, cat, and pigeon pictures.

Printed in Germany
by Amazon Distribution
GmbH, Leipzig